AN EVANS NOVEL OF THE WEST

BANDERA PASS

L.J. WASHBURN

M. EVANS & COMPANY, INC.   NEW YORK

Library of Congress Cataloging-in-Publication Data

Washburn, L. J.

  Bandera Pass / L. J. Washburn
    p.   cm. — (An Evans novel of the west)
  ISBN 0-87131-578-5
  I. Title. II. Series.
PS3573.A787B36 1989   89-11921
813'.54—dc20

M. Evans and Company, Inc.
216 East 49 Street
New York, New York 10017

Manufactured in the United States of America

9 8 7 6 5 4 3 2 1

For my father-in-law, Marion Reasoner, and two special friends, Dick and Bonnie Dickson.

Prologue

The chirping sound of crickets drifted in through the open window along with the warm summer air, a peaceful nighttime melody. But the man muttering and thrashing on the bed was anything but peaceful. From the looks of it, the dreams of Samuel Knight, sheriff of Bandera County, Texas, were haunted by ghosts or demons or both.

The nightmare had started simply enough. Sam was on his horse, riding through the hills north of the town of Bandera, toward the line of rugged peaks that separated the valley of the Medina River from that of the Guadalupe to the north. A sense of urgency gripped him, giving him a chill despite the warm sunshine of the day.

He was after a killer.

This was hardly the first time Sam Knight had stalked a wanted outlaw. He had been a lawman for many years, serving as sheriff in several central Texas counties before settling in Bandera. The man he was pursuing now, though, was maybe the worst of the lot, a vicious murderer.

Sam had to bring him to justice.

As he rode north, Sam saw Bandera Pass looming ahead of him. It was the only easy way of crossing the range of hills. Sam had heard the old-timers in the area talk about the Indian battle that had taken place in the pass in 1841, some thirty-three years earlier. This had been wild country then, and a group of Texas Rangers led by Captain Jack Hays had been ambushed in the pass by several hundred Comanches. After an hour of fierce, hand-to-hand fighting, the much smaller group of Rangers had routed the Indians. That battle had broken the back of their resistance to the white man's encroachment into this territory.

Bandera Pass was still a damn good place for an ambush, though.

Sam followed the trail to the pass, knowing that the outlaw he sought was up ahead somewhere. As he started up the slope that led through the opening, he cast nervous glances at the sides of the pass. They were steep, rocky, and brush covered, with plenty of places to hide. Sam's skin was crawling as he felt eyes watching him.

His quarry didn't try an ambush after all. Suddenly, a man stepped out onto the trail from behind a boulder. Sam reined in abruptly, his hand starting toward the gun holstered on his hip and then stopping when he saw that the man's hands were hanging loose and empty at his sides.

"Howdy, Sheriff," a mocking, somehow familiar voice drawled. "I reckon you finally caught up with me."

"I did," Sam said. "And I'm taking you back with me."

The man shook his head. "I'm not going anywhere." The sun had dropped close to the western horizon, throwing a gloomy mantle of shadow over the inside of the pass. Sam wished he could get a good look at the stranger confronting him to make sure he had the right man.

"And I say you're going with me," Sam said as he slowly swung down from the saddle. He kept his horse between himself and the stranger while he was doing it, so the man couldn't try any tricks. Once on the ground, Sam gently slapped his mount on the rump and waited as it stepped out of the way. His fingers dangled close to the butt of his Colt.

"You'll have to kill me to take me back," the man said.

Sam swallowed. His heart pounded heavily in his chest. But there was no backing down now. He had a job to do.

"If that's the way you want it," he said flatly.

The man stepped forward then, moving into the last rays of the setting sun as his hand darted toward his gun. Sam palmed out his own weapon, moving fast without rushing. The other man fired first, but he was too quick on the trigger. The slug whined past Sam, missing him cleanly. The sheriff lifted his gun, lining it on the figure, his finger tightening on the trigger just as he finally got a good look at the man's face.

Sam screamed as the gun in his hand blasted.

The face was his own.

And then it was gone, wiped out in a spray of blood and a gray haze of powdersmoke that drifted across the scene. As that image burned into his brain, Sam Knight bolted upright in his bed, still shouting. Beside him, his wife sat up and clutched at his arm, her soothing voice finally penetrating to his nightmare-fevered brain.

"It's the dream again, Sam," she told him. "Just the dream . . ."

Sam stared into the darkness of his bedroom and slowly came to realize that he was in his own home in Bandera, that his wife, Faye, was right beside him, that his daughter, Victoria, was in her own room down the hall. The town was calm and quiet and sleeping.

He took a deep breath and turned to Faye, patting her hand. "I'm all right," he said. "I'm all right now."

She leaned over and kissed his cheek. "Whatever that dream is, it must be terrible. Are you sure you don't want to tell me about it? It might help to talk about it."

Sam shook his head wordlessly. There was no way he could tell anyone about this, not even Faye.

She settled back down beside him and soon fell asleep again. Sam stretched out, put his hands behind his head, and stared up at the ceiling. He knew from experience that it would be a long time before he could go back to sleep.

There were beads of cold sweat on his forehead. He reached up, wiped them off, rubbed his hand on the tangled sheet.

The cold sweat would come back. It always did.

Chapter One

"You just don't know what it's like, Hank," Joe Casebolt said as he rubbed his swollen jaw. "It's the torments of the damned, that's what it is."

Hank Littleton smiled slightly. "I've had toothaches before, Joe," he said as he rode easy in the saddle behind the four prisoners they were taking back to Austin.

Casebolt shook his head and declared, "This ain't no ordinary toothache. This here's a real booger." He winced and hunched his shoulders from a fresh twinge of pain.

One of the prisoners twisted in his saddle and snapped over his shoulder, "Shut up, old man! Bad enough you're takin' us to jail without makin' us listen to your bellyachin' all the way!"

Casebolt straightened and glared at the outlaw. "You just hush, Kimbrough. I ain't goin' to put up with it, not the way I feel."

The prisoner just snorted and spat into the dust.

Hank's smile broadened into a grin. Casebolt and the Kimbrough brothers had been grousing at each other ever since they had left Georgetown. The trip to the capital would take several hours, and Hank expected that the arguing would continue most of the way.

He didn't mind. Even though this was his first assignment, he was already growing accustomed to the older man's irascibility.

Hank glanced down at the badge on his chest. It was worth a few minor irritations to wear that silver star on a silver circle, just as his father had done.

It was the badge of the Texas Rangers, and after years of inglorious disbandment after the Civil War, the best damn fighting force was back in the saddle again, and Hank Littleton was mighty proud to be one of them.

It beat the hell out of deputy sheriffing—and undertaking.

A tall, broad-shouldered young man with a thatch of sandy hair under his Stetson, Hank looked right at home on the back of a horse, a Henry rifle resting across the pommel in front of him. He had the reins in his left hand, his right rested on the rifle.

He had never been comfortable wearing the sober black suit of an undertaker. He could build a coffin with the best of them—his grandfather, Thomas, had taught him that, along with plenty of other things—but Hank had never had Thomas's ability to deal with grieving families.

When Hank had returned to San Saba after avenging his grandfather's murder, the citizens of the town had been quick to assume that he would take over Thomas's business. Hank was young at the time, only sixteen, but there was no one else to do the job. Hank's father, Enos, had his Ranger duties to attend to, and although he stayed in San Saba for a short while, the time had come when he had to leave. The War Between the States was at its height, and many of the men in Texas had left to fight for the Confederacy. That left the depleted group of Rangers to serve as the frontier's only line of defense against Indians and badmen.

And Hank, whether he wanted the job or not, became San Saba's undertaker.

That had lasted until several years after the end of the War, and Hank had hated every minute of it. Not only did he not like all the unpleasant details that went with the burying profession, he found that he was no businessman, either. By the time he gave it up, and managed to convince the townspeople that he meant what he said, half the people in San Saba owed him money. And Hank knew good and well he would never collect most of it either.

2

A couple of weeks after Congress had forced a new governor on the state, Enos came back through town.

"The Rangers are dead," he had told Hank in disgust. "That son-of-a-bitch Davis says he's goin' to do away with them."

Hank frowned and shook his head, unable to imagine Texas without the Rangers. "What'll we do for law and order?" he had asked his father.

"Davis is forming some sort of state police force," Enos had snorted. "I ain't havin' no part of it, though. Bunch of damned carpetbaggers and renegades, if you ask me."

"Then you can come back here and take over the business," Hank had said, trying not to let the feeling of relief that he was experiencing overwhelm him.

Enos just shook his head. "I'm on my way to Colorado," he said. "Figured I'd do me some mining, maybe get rich."

His father's plan had come as no surprise to Hank. Enos Littleton had always been a fiddlefooted sort, ever since Hank's mother had died many years earlier.

Enos had slapped Hank on the back as they stood on the front porch of the old house Thomas had built. "Why don't you come with me, son?" Enos had asked.

The invitation had made Hank feel all warm inside. After years of hardly ever seeing his father, the two of them had finally become close, and Hank thought long and hard about taking him up on the offer.

In the end, he had decided not to go to Colorado with his father. They had kept in touch, though, so Hank knew all about how Enos had wound up as a sheriff in a Rocky Mountain mining town full of hardcases and thieves. Once a man had carried a badge, Hank supposed, it was hard to get out of the habit.

He had packed a star himself for several years, working as a deputy sheriff in San Saba County. By then the undertaking business had been sold to a fellow from up at Goldthwaite who had been able to make a go of it.

Hank had had little trouble getting the deputy sheriff's job. A lot of folks still remembered what had happened during the War and even figured he was some sort of hero. Hank had never seen things quite that way, but he was willing to let people think whatever they wanted. A man named Zack Burchett was the sheriff, and he wasn't hard to work for, Hank discovered.

But putting up with Davis's State Police . . . Now that was a different story. Hank had never seen a more corrupt bunch in his life. Graft seemed to be a way of life with them, and between them and the outlaws they were supposed to catch, there was little to choose from. Hank had quickly grown tired of having run-ins with them when he was trying to do his job.

Like nearly everyone else in Texas, Hank had rejoiced when Davis was put out of office and Richard Coke was elected governor. Within days, the State Police had been disbanded, and the word had gone out to all former Rangers and anyone who was interested in becoming one.

The Texas Rangers were back.

Hank Littleton was on his way to Austin to sign up less than an hour after he read the story in San Saba's newspaper.

After taking the oath, he was assigned to the Special Force commanded by Captain Leander McNelly. There was a week of rather perfunctory training in horsemanship and gun handling, during which he had been introduced to his unofficial partner, a grizzled, middle-aged man named Joe Casebolt. Casebolt seemed to be little more than skin and bones, but there was a rawhide tough quality about him that came from surviving on the Texas frontier since the days before the Alamo and the battle for independence from Mexico. Hank was looking forward to working with him, figuring that there was quite a bit he could learn from a veteran like Casebolt.

Then they had both promptly sat on their butts for two months, waiting for McNelly to give them something to do.

That wait had come to an end the day before, when McNelly called them into his office and told them to ride up to Georgetown to pick up some prisoners. "The Kimbrough brothers," the mild-looking commander had said quietly. "They robbed the First State Bank yesterday and fled north, but the authorities in Georgetown apprehended them. All you need to do, gentlemen, is to return them here to the Austin city jail."

Now, as he and Casebolt rode along behind the Kimbrough brothers, Casebolt muttered thickly, "I knew when I got up this mornin' that this was goin' to be a bad 'un. I should'a filled up a sock with sassafras leaves and tied it around my jaw."

Another of the Kimbroughs hipped around in his saddle and said, "It would've done more good *in* your mouth."

"You shut up, too," Casebolt snapped. Hank tried not to laugh, knowing that the older Ranger would be offended if he thought Hank was making light of his toothache.

For outlaws who had pulled off several successful robberies, the Kimbroughs didn't look like a particularly threatening bunch. All of them were scrawny and undersized, from Cecil, the oldest at thirty, to Lucius, who was not quite twenty yet. In between were William and Doyle. With the exception of Lucius, all of them had scraggly dark beards. Their hats were battered and disreputable, their clothes patched several times over. The only things they had seemed to take good care of were their boots and holsters and saddles. And their guns; Hank had their unloaded revolvers stored in his saddlebags.

Despite Casebolt's grouchiness and the surly attitude of the prisoners, Hank was enjoying himself. He had never been to this part of the state until he and Casebolt had ridden up to Georgetown the day before. The Texas hill country rose to the west, a series of rocky ridges covered with trees and brush. The Colorado River, along with several other smaller streams, cut through dozens of rugged canyons on the way from the high country to the Gulf. To the east was prairie land. The few hills that were there were gently rolling slopes. Hank took it all in.

The six riders were approaching the southern fork of the San Gabriel River. The road dropped down a hill into the river valley and wound along beside the stream for a couple of miles before it reached the ford. The river was narrow and shallow there, with a firm rocky bed, no trouble to cross. The south bank was much steeper than the northern one, and its heights were choked with brush. The river twisted and turned, so that it was hard to see more than a few hundred yards up or down its path.

As the riders started across the river, Cecil Kimbrough glanced over his shoulder again at the two Rangers, an ugly grin on his face. "You boys are just plain dumb fools," he said. "You really think our cousins are going to let you take us all the way to Austin?"

Casebolt frowned. "Didn't know you had any cousins," he said. "Wouldn't figure polecats would know the difference, anyway."

"What do you mean, polecats?" Lucius asked, looking baffled.

"They'd have to be, was they related to you, boy," Casebolt replied. He started to chuckle, then winced again and raised his hand to his jaw.

Hank saw the flicker of light and knew that Cecil Kimbrough should have kept his gloating to himself.

"Watch it, Joe!" he shouted as he snapped the Henry up and kicked his feet out of the stirrups. There was a sharp crack as Hank dropped from the saddle and landed in the shallow water. Lead sang past his ear as he whipped the rifle to his shoulder and sighted on the small puff of smoke he spotted upriver.

Hank fired four shots as quick as he could work the rifle's lever. Their thunder rolled across the river and echoed back from the south bank. A high-pitched scream blended in with the echoes. A shape pitched forward out of the brush on the riverbank and fell loosely down the slope.

Cecil Kimbrough let out a yell and dug his boot heels into the flanks of his horse. The animal leaped forward. The others galloped after him, all four of the outlaw brothers making a desperate bid for the south bank of the river and freedom.

More shots crackled from upstream, and slugs kicked up little geysers of water from the river's surface. Hank grabbed the reins of his nervous horse and pulled it back. The closest cover was on the northern bank. Casebolt was yelling angrily as he wheeled his mount around and headed in the same direction.

"We rode right into a goddamn ambush!" Casebolt shouted. He clawed out his Colt and fired upstream as several men on horseback came pounding around a bend in the river. The bushwhackers charged at Hank and Casebolt, shooting as they came.

Hank reached the northern bank and splashed up onto the rocky shore. He threw a glance at the fleeing Kimbrough brothers, then snapped two quick shots at the attacking riders. Those had to be some of the cousins Cecil Kimbrough had mentioned, and the men hidden in the brush probably were, too. One of the slugs flying around hit a rock near Hank and ricocheted off with an eerie sound. Hank dove behind an outcropping of stone.

The Kimbroughs had almost reached the south bank by now, he saw as he looked in that direction again. Hank grimaced. His first job as a Ranger, and he had botched it. The outlaw brothers were going to escape unless he stopped them somehow in the next few seconds.

Hank twisted around on the hard ground to fire across the river, ignoring for the moment all the bullets whining around him. He might have been able to drop one or two of the Kimbroughs, he knew, but then the others would get away. He sighted instead on the horse being ridden by Cecil Kimbrough, who was in the lead.

The Henry blasted. Somehow the bullet threaded its way among the three galloping horses in the rear and struck Cecil's mount just behind the right foreleg, bursting on through to the animal's heart and killing it instantly. The horse dropped like a stone, sending up a huge splash, and Cecil went flying through the air.

Unable to avoid the fallen horse, William, Doyle, and Lucius, in a tangle of hoof-flailing horseflesh, went down as well.

That would slow the Kimbroughs down, Hank thought as he turned his attention back to the other men. Casebolt had dropped from his own horse and was crouched beside Hank now, emptying his Colt at the ambushers. The boom of the percussion revolver was deafening at this range. Hank lined his sights on the charging riders and began to fire. There were eight cartridges remaining in his rifle after downing Cecil Kimbrough's horse, and he loosed all of them at the attackers in a matter of seconds. Three men went flying out of their saddles. The others reined in abruptly and started trying to turn their mounts.

Hank raised himself onto his knees and pulled out the pistol holstered on his hip. It was a brand-new Colt Single Action Army, bought when he had arrived in Austin and joined the Rangers. He had already heard several men refer to it as a Peacemaker. Never as good with a handgun as he was with a rifle, Hank had practiced until he could handle the Colt fairly well. He squeezed off two shots now, adding his support to Casebolt's fire.

"We got 'em on the run, Hank!" Casebolt whooped as he emptied his revolver. "They weren't expectin' to run into no sharpshooter like you."

The losses they had suffered had evidently convinced the would-be rescuers to abandon the attempt, Hank saw. The three wounded men who had been knocked off their horses were lying in the streambed, trying to keep their heads above water. Hank looked toward the Kimbrough brothers again and saw that they were trying to get their horses back on their feet.

The rifle fire from the hidden men seemed to have stopped. No doubt they had taken off, too, when they saw their companions being dropped so efficiently. Knowing he was still taking a chance, Hank stood up and hurried over to his horse. Swinging up into the saddle, he sent the animal splashing into the San Gabriel again.

"You fellas had better just forget it," Hank said a moment later as he rode up to the disorganized Kimbroughs, his Colt still in his hand and ready. "Those cousins of yours have headed for the tall and uncut, leastways those of them who still can."

Cecil Kimbrough was lying on the bank, clutching his leg and moaning. "Dammit, Ranger," he grated, "I think I broke my leg when you shot that horse out from under me!"

"Doyle's worse off than that," Lucius said in a choked voice. The youngest of the brothers moved aside, and Hank could see Doyle Kimbrough lying half in and half out of the river. His face was in the water, but he made no effort to move it. The angle of his neck struck Hank as strange, and then he knew that Doyle was dead.

"It happened when our horses went down," Lucius said, swallowing a sob. "His horse fell right on top of him. He never had a chance, dammit!"

"I'm sorry," Hank said softly, and he meant it. Lucius didn't seem to hear him.

Casebolt rode up a moment later, herding three new prisoners in front of him. One of the men had a bullet-shattered shoulder and was very pale. The other two had suffered less serious wounds. One had a bullet crease on the side, the other a hole in the fleshy part of his thigh. With a broad grin on his face, Casebolt said, "Looks like we got us some new prisoners to go to Austin with, Hank."

"Round Rock's not far. We'd better stop there and see if we can get them patched up. Can you take care of them?"

"You bet," Casebolt replied, hefting the big Colt in his hand. "They ain't got no more fight left."

"I'll go try to scare up some horses, then," Hank said.

Keeping an eye out in case of any of the other bushwhackers decided to make another try at them, Hank rode upstream and found a couple of the riderless horses. He brought them back to the ford. The horses that the Kimbroughs had been riding had not been hurt in their wild fall, which was a stroke of luck. That gave them five mounts for the six prisoners—and Doyle Kimbrough's body.

Lucius and William tied Doyle onto the back of one horse, then doubled up with two cousins after helping Cecil mount up. Cecil was still complaining about his leg, and Hank saw that it did look broken.

Then the group started south again, following the road up the slope of the bank and emerging onto rolling prairie again.

Casebolt kept his gun out. He said to Hank, "I think I'll keep this hogleg handy, happen any of these varmints tries to get tricky again."

"I don't think they will," Hank replied. "I think they've had enough for today."

After a few minutes, Casebolt asked, "What do you think Cap'n McNelly's goin' to say when he sees these fellers? He sent us after four prisoners, and we're fetchin' him back six, seven countin' the dead one."

"I reckon maybe he'll think we earned our pay."

"Say, where'd you learn to shoot a rifle like that? I seen you practicin' in Austin and knew you could hit a target, but I never saw nobody make a shot like the one that dropped that lead hoss."

Hank smiled as he thought about his grandfather, who had been good but not spectacular with both rifle and pistol, and his father, whose speed with a six-gun was blinding. "I guess that was what came up when it was my turn," he said. "A gift, I reckon you could call it."

"Well, it's a hell of a handy one out here. You best thank whoever give it to you."

Hank looked down again at the Ranger star on his chest. His father and grandfather had worn badges, too.

He hoped he was thanking them by wearing this one.

Chapter Two

Cecil Kimbrough's leg was indeed broken, the doctor in Round Rock confirmed. He set it and splinted it, Kimbrough howling in pain throughout the procedure, then bound up the shoulder of the other seriously wounded man and strapped his arm to his side to keep it from moving around. The two remaining minor wounds were quickly taken care of, and Hank and Casebolt and the prisoners were on the trail again.

The group reached Austin in the late afternoon and drew quite a few curious looks from the people on the streets as they rode downtown to the jail. The Travis County sheriff came out of the stone building to see what the commotion was about and gnawed on his bushy moustache in surprise.

"You Rangers always bring back more than you were sent after?" he finally asked dryly.

"Just sometimes," Casebolt replied. He jerked a calloused thumb at the extra prisoners. "These boys are cousins to the Kimbroughs, or at least so Cecil claims. Tried to bust 'em loose up north of Round Rock. Doyle Kimbrough got his neck broke in the ruckus."

"Well, we'll take good care of them," the sheriff replied, motioning for some of his deputies to get the prisoners down from the horses and into cells. The body was untied from the horse so that it could be carried to the undertaker's. The lawman cuffed his hat back and looked up at Hank and Casebolt. He went on, "Tell McNelly I appreciate him sending you boys."

Hank nodded. "Sure thing, Sheriff." He turned his horse and headed toward Ranger headquarters with Casebolt.

The offices of the Texas Rangers Special Force were housed in a government building not far from the state capitol. The Colonial Capitol, as it was called, was a large, imposing limestone structure, three stories tall and surmounted by a high dome. A lawn with three terraces led down to the street. Altogether, it was a magnificent seat of government for the Lone Star State.

The building that housed the Ranger offices was not nearly as impressive, and neither was the slender, pallid man who looked up from behind his desk to greet Hank and Casebolt.

Captain Leander McNelly said, "Good evening, gentlemen." He pushed one of the stacks of paperwork in front of him to the side and laced his fingers together on the desktop. "I trust you were successful in your mission."

"Yes, sir," Casebolt replied as he took his hat off and held it in both hands. "The Kimbrough brothers are in the county jail, 'cept the one that's dead, of course. And we brung in a few extra prisoners, too."

McNelly was silent for a moment as he digested this information, then he said, "There was an escape attempt?"

"Yes, sir. Some of the Kimbroughs' cousins hit us at the San Gabriel ford, north of Round Rock. Doyle Kimbrough's hoss wound up fallin' on him. Busted his neck right in two. We captured three of the fellers who ambushed us and brung them with us."

"I see," McNelly nodded. He switched his attention to Hank. "Do you have anything to add to Mr. Casebolt's statement, Mr. Littleton?"

Hank shook his head. "No, sir. It happened just the way Joe told it."

"Very well. I always trust the judgment of my men until I have reason to do otherwise. And I've heard good things about both of you." McNelly picked up a pen, dipped it into the inkwell, and scratched something on one of the papers on the desk. Without looking up from his writing, he went on, "I'll want a written report on the matter from both of you."

"Aw, Cap'n, you know I ain't much on writin'," Casebolt groaned. "I can get my name down all right, but that's about all."

"How about you, Mr. Littleton?"

"I can write," Hank answered a little stiffly.

"Fine. You take care of the report, and both you and Ranger Casebolt can sign it."

"Yes, sir," Hank acknowledged. He started backing toward the door of the office, thinking that McNelly was through with them. Casebolt edged along with him.

"Just a moment," McNelly said sharply. "I have something else to discuss with you."

Hank and Casebolt exchanged a worried glance, but they stayed where they were. McNelly kept writing, and in the awkward silence that stretched out over the next couple of minutes, Hank wondered what the devil the captain wanted.

McNelly was a good man; nobody doubted that. He had originally been a captain in the State Police, one of the few honest members of that hated force. In the few months since his appointment, McNelly had made it clear on several occasions that he was not going to ask his men to do anything he himself was not willing to undertake. Captain or not, whenever he could get away from all the paperwork that went with his job, he hit the saddle and rode out into action with the rest of the Rangers.

His pale, thin face gave some hint that he was not in the best of health, but from the things that Hank had heard about the man, McNelly didn't let that slow him down. But just as McNelly demanded a great deal from himself, he also expected quite a bit from his men. As he and Casebolt waited for McNelly to finish, Hank had a feeling that the captain had another job for them already.

"There," McNelly said, sliding the paper aside and replacing the pen in its stand. "I wanted to get those thoughts down while they were fresh in my mind. Now, I have another assignment for you gentlemen—" He broke off and frowned at Casebolt. "Mr. Casebolt, what the deuce is wrong with your jaw?"

Casebolt lifted a hand to rub the jaw, a pained expression on his face.

12

"Got a bad tooth, Cap'n," he said. "It swole up on me last night and hurt so bad today it durn near blinded me. I was sorta hopin' we might have a little time off so's I could find me a tooth doctor."

"From the looks of it, it does need attending to," McNelly agreed. "But you'll have to take care of it this evening. You and Mr. Littleton will be riding out first thing in the morning."

Casebolt grimaced. Hank took a deep breath and nodded, saying, "Yes, sir. Where are we heading?"

"The sheriff of Bexar County has requested our assistance in tracking down a gang of outlaws that has been plaguing his jurisdiction." McNelly consulted another document. "They've held up several stage-coaches and also robbed the express office in San Antonio. There's been shooting during some of these crimes, and three men have been killed. Are you familiar with the area around San Antonio, Mr. Littleton?"

Hank shook his head. "No, sir, I'm afraid not."

"Don't worry, Cap'n," Casebolt put in. "I know that country. We won't have any trouble findin' our way around."

"Very good, Mr. Casebolt. Several witnesses have identified some of the criminals, including the man who appears to be the leader of the gang." A frown passed over McNelly's face. "His name is Isom Whitaker."

Hank didn't say anything for a moment as the surprise hit him. He knew that name, knew it all too well. Finally, he said with hesitation, "I ran into a fella named Whitaker who was in the State Police . . ."

"One and the same man," McNelly confirmed. "Whitaker was under my command at one time. I never had a very high opinion of the man's ethics, but he was quite efficient at his job."

"He came into San Saba County and gunned down some local boys who were just trying to get by," Hank said tightly.

McNelly stared up at him. "Those men were stealing from some of the landholders up there, if I remember the circumstances correctly."

Hank didn't flinch from the intense gaze this time. "Those so-called landholders were nothing but no-good carpetbaggers, Captain. And the men Whitaker hunted down and killed all had families to take care of. He didn't have any right to go after them—"

"He was a member of the State Police," McNelly pointed out.

"And he never even gave them a chance to surrender." Bitterness

13

was plain to hear in Hank's voice. He ignored the warning looks Casebolt was giving him and went on, "Whitaker and his men just rode up to them on the street and shot them down like dogs."

"As I said, I never cared for Whitaker's ethics," McNelly replied coldly. "I wouldn't have a man like that in the Rangers, and you know it, Mr. Littleton."

Hank nodded curtly, accepting the reprimand. "Yes, sir. Reckon I do."

"As I was saying, Isom Whitaker appears to be the leader of this band of outlaws. Evidently he crossed the line to the wrong side of the law when the State Police were disbanded, and he took some other former officers with him. Several of the gang have been identified as having been members of the State Police, while others are thought to be simple hardcases. I'm charging you two men with the responsibility of ending their depredations."

"What if they light a shuck out of Bexar when they hear the Rangers are after 'em?" Casebolt asked.

McNelly's reply was simple: "Go after them."

Casebolt was shaking his head when he and Hank walked out of Ranger headquarters a few minutes later. "I wouldn't talk back to the cap'n like that, was I you, son," he said. "He may look like a school-teacher, but I've heard tell he can stay in the saddle all day and all night and still whip his weight in bobcats."

"I know," Hank nodded. "But you never saw folks you'd grown up with gunned down, and the men who did it standing over them and laughing."

"I've seen worse things, Hank," Casebolt replied. "That Whitaker feller's an owlhoot now. We'll catch up to him and even the score. You wait and see." He winced for at least the hundredth time that day. "Damn! Let's see if we can find somebody who'll take care of this tooth."

They turned down Congress Avenue, nodding and returning the greetings of several other Rangers who were ambling along the board-walk. Dusk was settling over the city now, leaving a red glow in the sky behind the capitol at the top of the hill, and tinny music was beginning to float out into the street. There was quite a bit of traffic on the broad, dusty avenue, mostly men on horseback with a few wagons and buggies mixed in. At the foot of the hill, the Colorado River drifted lazily toward the Gulf.

Casebolt stopped at the entrance of a false-fronted limestone building and said, "Here's what we need."

Looking past him, Hank saw that the place was a saloon. "I thought you were looking for a dentist."

"Rufe Jonas can tell me where to find one. Hell, he knows ever'body in town."

Casebolt pushed through the batwings and led the way into the saloon. It was fancier than most Hank had been in, with a real mahogany bar and circular chandeliers that hung from the ceiling beams. There was a long gilt-framed mirror behind the bar, and situated on the opposite wall so that it would be reflected in the mirror's surface was a painting of a nude woman reclining on a sofa. The brass rail at the bottom of the bar reflected light from the chandeliers. The backbar on either side of the mirror was lined with what seemed like hundreds of bottles of liquor. A dozen tables were scattered around the floor; in an open space next to a piano the saloon's customers could dance with the bar girls. In the back of the room were several more tables, these with felt-covered tops. The gamblers held court here, dealing poker and faro and blackjack. At the end of the bar, looking out over the big room with an expression of pride on his face, stood a large man in a dusty black suit.

Casebolt strode up to this man and thrust out his hand. "Rufe!" he said. "How you doin', you old bastard?"

Rufe Jonas lost his prideful look for a moment and frowned at the Ranger. Then recognition dawned on his flushed features and he said, "Joe Casebolt! I thought they must have hung you ten years ago for a horse thief."

Casebolt jerked a thumb at the badge on his vest. "Nope, I'm on the side of law and order, Rufe. I hope you're keepin' your nose clean. I'd pure-dee hate to have to arrest you."

Jonas laughed. "That'll be the day! Why don't you and your young friend have a drink?"

"Sure." Casebolt put his hands on the bar and inclined his head for Hank to join him. "Two beers," he told the bartender who came hurrying up to take his order.

Hank was hungrier than he was thirsty, but the beer was cool and good. He sipped from the mug and listened to Casebolt and Jonas hooraw each other as they talked over old times. From the sound of it, the two men had fought all the Indians and Mexican renegades and loved all the women in the State of Texas.

The saloon was doing a brisk trade. The space along the bar was mostly filled, and there were only one or two empty tables. A bald-headed piano player was making up with enthusiasm what he lacked in talent, and in the back of the room the clink of glasses blended with the shuffle of cards and the low voices of the men sitting in on the games.

"How long you been in Austin City, Joe?" the saloonkeeper asked.

"Just a short spell," Casebolt replied. "I rode down from Fort Worth to join up with the Rangers."

"You've been here that long and haven't been in to see me?" Jonas sounded offended.

Casebolt shrugged. "We been busy," he lied. "Cap'n McNelly seems to think that me and my partner are the only fellers he's got who can handle anything. By the way, this here's Hank Littleton, Rufe. He's a hell of a Ranger and the damnedest shot with a Henry rifle you ever did see."

The big man shook hands with Hank. "Glad to meet you, young fellow. You pay attention to everything Joe here tells you, and you'll stay alive."

"That's what he keeps telling me, Mr. Jonas," Hank said with a grin.

Jonas turned back to Casebolt. "Say, you'd never figure who's here, Joe. And she's been just pining away for you, too. She's going to be mighty glad to see you."

Casebolt frowned. "Who're you talkin' about, Rufe?"

By way of answer, Jonas turned his head and called across the room, "Dovey! Come over here."

Casebolt paled, then drained his beer mug in one gulp. "Dovey?" he said in a hollow voice. The way he glanced nervously around, Hank thought he had the look of a man looking for a bolt hole.

A blond woman in a tight, frilly dress came sweeping up to the bar, her heavily made-up face breaking into a smile when she saw Casebolt. "Joe!" she exclaimed. "You came back to me! I knew you would, sooner or later."

16

Hank turned and looked in the mirror behind the bar so Casebolt wouldn't see the big grin on his face. The older Ranger stammered and looked uncomfortable as Dovey linked arms with him and led him away from the bar. Casebolt glanced over his shoulder, obviously searching for help, but even though Hank saw the look in the mirror, he kept his attention on his mug of beer.

Casebolt got himself into this, Hank thought with a chuckle. He could damn well get himself out.

It was full dark by the time Casebolt managed to extricate himself from Dovey and leave Rufe Jonas's saloon with Hank following him. On the boardwalk outside, Casebolt drew a deep breath and then grimaced as the air hit his bad tooth. Hank asked dryly, "Did you find out where to get your tooth worked on?"

"Rufe said there's a jaw-cracker over on Guadalupe Street," Casebolt replied. "Let's get over there. This tooth is painin' me somethin' fierce."

"Reckon Miss Dovey might've worked on it for free," Hank commented as he fell into step beside Casebolt.

"Hank . . . shut up."

"Why, sure, Joe," Hank replied in mock innocence.

It took them only a few minutes to find the dentist's office on Guadalupe Street. It was on the upper floor of a building, above a hardware store. A flight of stairs led up the outside of the building to the entrance. Hank and Casebolt climbed it only to find the door locked. Casebolt banged his fist on it several times, but there was no answer.

"Dammit!" he growled. "This feller's supposed to be painless, but he ain't goin' to do me no good if he ain't here." The older Ranger sighed. "Come on. We'll see if we can find a barber to yank this tooth."

A half-hour's search up and down the streets surrounding the capitol revealed that all the barbershops were closed down for the night, too. Casebolt stopped in a tavern and bought a bottle of whiskey, strictly for pain-killing purposes, he solemnly declared. "What kind of a town is this?" he said as he swigged from the bottle and glared. "Ever'thin' shuts down soon's it gets dark."

"The saloons don't," Hank pointed out.

"Reckon that's true enough." Casebolt took another drink, then slapped Hank on the back. "Come on, son. We might's well go on back to Rufe's place. That gal Dovey's been known to deaden a few pains in her time."

Hank shook his head. "I think I'll head back to the barracks and try to get some sleep. We've got a long ride to San Antonio in the morning."

"You sure? I reckon Dovey could scare up a gal for you, too. You ain't as handsome as me, of course, but I don't imagine the gals run an' hide from you, neither."

"That's all right, Joe. I'm pretty tired."

Casebolt nodded. "Gettin' shot at does that to some fellers. All right, son, you go on. I'll see you in the mornin' at sunup, and we'll be off to San Antone."

Casebolt went on down the street, drinking from the bottle and wincing. Hank watched him go, then turned toward the Ranger barracks. He was glad Casebolt hadn't insisted that he return to Jonas's saloon. Hank liked a drink now and then, and he had flirted with his share of bar girls, but a night of carousing wasn't what he wanted now. He wasn't sure that sleep was, either.

He had known violence at an early age. He had killed men when he was little more than a boy himself. During his time as a deputy sheriff, he had traded lead with outlaws.

But today, on his first assignment as a Ranger, death had jumped out at him again. He wondered if it was going to be like that for the rest of his life—folks coming at him with guns, trying to kill him, forcing him to kill them.

He thought about that for a long time as he walked through the quiet Austin night.

Chapter Three

The International and Great Northern Railway train was southbound, headed for Corpus Christi and the Gulf of Mexico. It had pulled out of the station in San Antonio a short while earlier and left the southern fringes of the city only minutes before the men on horseback appeared beside the tracks. The engineer spotted them, sensed that they meant trouble, and lunged for the brake.

The fuse sputtering between two of the ties finally burned down, and a keg of blasting powder buried in the roadbed exploded with a huge thump. Dirt and gravel were hurled high in the air. The explosion went off about a hundred yards in front of the locomotive. All along the cars, the brakemen leaned heavily on their wheels in a desperate bid to bring the plunging train to a halt. The screech of the brakes blended with the surprised yells of the passengers and crew.

Fifty yards ahead, Isom Whitaker pulled in the reins of his startled horse as it danced around nervously. The train finally shuddered to a halt only a few feet before reaching the torn-up tracks.

Whitaker's sunburned face split in a grin. "All right, boys!" he called to the riders with him. "Let's take 'em!" He put the spurs to his horse and sent it galloping down the tracks, pulling out his Smith & Wesson as he rode. The long tails of the duster he wore flapped behind him.

The people on board the train would be too shaken up to know what was going on for a few minutes. By the time they did, Whitaker and his men would be in control.

There were eight men with him. As they flashed past the steaming locomotive, one of the riders reined in and dropped from the saddle. He bounced up the steps into the cab of the engine and triggered a shot as the fireman picked himself up off the floor and reached for his shovel. The bullet smacked into the blade of the shovel and knocked it out of the fireman's hand.

"Hold it, mister!" the robber ordered. "You, too," he growled to the engineer. "Both you fellas just stay still, and you'll live through this just fine."

The two crewmen did as they were told. The savage grin on the outlaw's leathery face was proof enough that he would shoot them without thinking twice about it.

At the same time, others in Whitaker's gang converged on the three passenger cars. Two men entered each car, guns drawn and ready. There were no shots, though, no opposition from the people on board. Whitaker's men took the travelers by surprise, getting the drop on them. In each car the scene was repeated. One man covered the passengers while the other man collected wallets and money belts and jewelry.

Whitaker and the remaining member of the gang headed for the express car. The outlaw leader barked, "Get it open, Brian!" as he hauled his horse to a stop beside the car.

Brian, who was considerably younger than Whitaker, leaped from his saddle to the platform at the rear of the car, his pistol in hand. Standing to one side of the door, he blasted two shots into the lock. The slugs smashed the latch, and the outlaw was able to drive a booted foot into the door and send it slamming open. He ducked back as a shotgun boomed inside the car. Buckshot whipped through the air, several of the pellets ricocheting off the railing around the platform.

Whitaker leaned in from the other side, firing at an angle into the car. The gun in his hand cracked three times before he pulled back on the reins and whirled the horse out of the way of any possible return fire. The other man, who had dodged back onto the steps on the far side of the platform, stretched his arm forward and sent two more bullets into the car.

Then Whitaker and his companion waited, their guns ready. There was only silence now in the express car.

Both men knew that only one barrel of the express messenger's shotgun had been fired. If the man was playing possum, stepping into that doorway was a good way to get a bellyful of buckshot. That was the only way into the car, though. The big sliding door on the side would be fastened inside with an iron bar. It could be blown open, but that would take time and more blasting powder, neither of which Whitaker and his men had.

Already the explosion and the shooting that had followed might be bringing help from San Antonio.

Whitaker caught the eye of the younger man and nodded curtly. The man's lean, bearded face broke into a grin of understanding. He knew the chance he would be taking, but a gleam of natural recklessness sparkled in his blue eyes. Pausing for a moment, he took more cartridges from his shell belt and thumbed them into the revolver.

Then he stepped up to the door and went through it quickly.

Seconds later, he reappeared, the grin on his face even wider. "The fella's dead."

Whitaker nodded in satisfaction. He swung down from his horse, glancing up the train as he did so. None of his other men had shown up yet, which meant they were still busy in the passenger cars. Whitaker hadn't heard any gunfire except for one shot from the engine and the shooting that he and Brian had done back here. Everything was still under control, he thought.

Bounding up the steps to the platform, Whitaker followed Brian into the express car. He barely spared a glance at the body of the messenger, sprawled face down in a pool of blood. One of the shots that had been thrown into the car had done its job. Whitaker turned his attention instead to the bags of mail and the heavy iron safe.

"Load up those bags," he ordered his partner. "We'll go through them later and see if there's anything valuable."

Brian nodded and hefted two of the bags, grunting with the effort. He took them out and tied one on each of the horses, then returned for the other two bags.

Whitaker knelt in front of the safe. Back in the days when he was a member of the State Police, he had worked several times with Wells Fargo, and he still had contacts in their offices around the state. It had cost him more than he wanted to pay to learn the combination of this safe, but it was going to be worth it if the tip he had received was right. He licked his lips as he spun the dial on the safe.

Working the combination took only seconds, and then Whitaker grunted in satisfaction as he twisted the handle and pulled the door of the safe open. Inside were several canvas bags. He reached in and pulled one out, grinning as he felt the tightly packed bundles inside. Opening the bag, he looked inside and saw the green of currency.

Then, moving quickly, he took all the bags out and stacked them on the floor. There were six of them, all stamped FIRST CATTLEMAN'S BANK OF FORT WORTH. The man who had told Whitaker about this money shipment had been right.

There was nothing else of value in the safe. Brian came up and knelt beside Whitaker, eyeing the sacks of greenbacks. "Those mailbags are loaded," the younger man said. "Is this the rest of it?"

"This is what we came for," Whitaker confirmed. He picked up two of the money bags and stuffed them inside his shirt. Brian gathered up the others, hanging on to one and taking the others outside to distribute to the other men.

Whitaker paused before leaving the express car. This was the best job they had pulled so far. Everything had gone smoothly, and they would clear at least twenty thousand from those money bags, plus whatever else they found in the mail and stole from the passengers.

Whitaker took a deep breath. He was a tall man in his forties, broad in the chest and shoulders, with long, powerful arms. His hat was pushed back on thick, curly red hair, and he had the fair, easily burned skin that went with it. His pale gray eyes were intelligent and, despite the quick grin that was habitual with him, usually cold. He had enjoyed being a State Policeman, had thrived on the power that came with his position, even if he had been forced to work with a bunch of freed slaves under his command. Being on the other side of the law was even better, though.

Before he was through, he had vowed that his name was going to be even bigger than those of Frank and Jesse James, and so was his fortune.

Those were the things he thought about at a moment like this, when a successful job had just been completed. They raced through his mind in a split second. There was no more time to waste; they still had to make their getaway.

Distracted by thoughts of the glories of his outlaw career, Whitaker failed to notice the feeble movements of the express messenger on the floor behind him.

Somehow, despite the horrible wound in his chest and the blood he had lost, the man had found the strength to drag himself back to consciousness. He lifted his head, blinking eyes that focused long enough for him to make out the shape of the duster-clad figure. The messenger's brain sent a command for his arm to move, and after what seemed like an hour, it finally did. His fingers closed over the stock of the shotgun he had dropped. He started to lift the heavy weapon, his finger clawing for the trigger.

Whitaker heard the scrape of the gun against the planks of the floor. He whirled around, his instincts taking over. He had holstered his gun when he knelt to open the safe, but now his hand flashed to the pistol, brushing back the duster with practiced ease and closing around the walnut butt of the gun. Whitaker saw the wavering muzzles of the greener turning toward him and threw himself to the side as he drew. The shotgun boomed, its thunderous discharge deafening in the close confines of the express car.

Buckshot smashed past him, one of the pellets burning the back of his left hand. Whitaker was too close to the messenger for the load to have spread out any, and his desperate dodge away from the barrels had saved him. Whitaker jerked his own gun up and fired twice, the heavy slugs smashing into the messenger's head. The shotgun clattered to the floor again, this time for good.

Brian appeared in the doorway, an anxious look on his face and his gun up and ready. "What the hell . . . ?" he asked breathlessly.

Whitaker jerked his head toward the body of the messenger. "I thought you said he was dead!" he snapped.

"I thought he was!"

Whitaker pushed past the younger man. "Come on. We don't have time to argue about it now."

He saw that the other members of the gang were waiting on their horses beside the express car. Under the guns of two of the outlaws, the train's conductor, engineer, firemen, and brakemen stood nearby.

"Any trouble with the passengers or crew?" Whitaker asked as he mounted his horse.

One of the other men grinned and said, "They was all meek as li'l lambs, boss."

"Good," Whitaker grunted. He faced the train crew and went on, "You boys just stay right here and don't cause any trouble, you'll be fine. I reckon somebody back in San Antone probably heard the shooting, so you'll have company pretty quick now."

"You son-of-a-bitch!" the conductor said impulsively, his anger getting the best of him. "What happened to Stevens?"

"The express man?" Whitaker shook his head. "He wasn't as smart as you fellas are going to be."

"You killed him, didn't you?" the conductor demanded.

"He didn't give me a lot of choice," Whitaker replied icily.

Suddenly, one of the other outlaws yelled, "Boss! Riders comin'!"

Whitaker looked up and gave a heartfelt curse. He could see the group almost a mile down the tracks, dust boiling up from the pounding hooves of their horses. The outlaws had waited just a little too long.

"Let's go!" he cried as he wheeled his horse around. He put the spurs to his animal to send it galloping away from the train.

At that moment, the conductor leaped forward, reaching up to grab at Whitaker's coat. The outlaw leader felt himself being jerked backward and cursed again. If he was unhorsed, that would slow them down enough for the posse to catch up to them. He twisted in the saddle and tried to get a shot at the conductor, who was hanging on for dear life.

Before the trainman could pull Whitaker from his horse, a gun appeared in the hand of the outlaw called Brian. The Colt barked, and the slug took the conductor in the shoulder, smashing bone and knocking him loose from Whitaker. The man screamed thinly as he fell to the ground.

Whitaker spurred his horse again, and this time it bounded forward into a run. The others were right behind him as he galloped away from the train. Whitaker cast a glance over his shoulder. The riders from San Antonio were closer now, but the gang still had the lead to give them the slip, Whitaker thought.

He looked over at Brian, who was riding hard beside him, leaning over the neck of his horse. "Thanks!" Whitaker called over the rush of wind that slapped at them.

Brian grinned and reached up to pat the lump that the money bag made inside his shirt. Whitaker knew what he meant. Brian would be well paid for helping to keep his leader alive. The group had pulled some profitable jobs since Whitaker had formed it.

Pushing their mounts for all they were worth, the outlaws gradually pulled away from the pursuers behind them. Their horses were good ones, picked for their speed and stamina, and the posse couldn't keep up. Isom Whitaker and his gang were going to make another successful getaway.

They rode northwest over rolling prairie toward the hill country, that rugged area of central Texas where a hundred outlaw gangs could hide in the rocky valleys. San Antonio and the surrounding territory had been the scene of several of their holdups, and now it was time to move on.

But Texas was a big place, Whitaker thought as he enjoyed the feel of warm sun and cool breezes and stolen money in his pocket. Yes, sir, a mighty big place.

And before he got through, he was going to loot every bit of it.

Chapter Four

Hank supposed he had seen more miserable-looking men than Casebolt, but he couldn't remember just where or when. The older Ranger was leaning against the wall of the stable when Hank walked in. His eyes were closed and his hand gripped his jaw. Every so often a little moan would come from him.

"Reckon we should've looked for another dentist last night," Hank said. "Doesn't look like Miss Dovey did your tooth a whole lot of good."

Casebolt cracked one eye and bleakly regarded Hank. Trying to move his mouth as little as possible, he growled, "Shut up, boy."

Hank grinned and went to saddle his horse. While he was at it, he got Casebolt's mount ready to ride as well.

Dawn was just breaking over Austin when Hank led the horses out of the stable where most of the Rangers kept their mounts. The rising sun reflected redly on the surface of the Colorado River a block away. Despite the early hour, there were quite a few people on the streets, and Hank had a feeling that if he was to walk up Congress Avenue, he'd find Captain McNelly already at work in his office.

Casebolt followed him out of the stable, still holding his jaw and grumbling. Hank asked, "You want to get some breakfast before we start out?"

"I ain't sure I can eat with this damn tooth actin' up, but I reckon I'd best give it a try. Man can't do without food, no matter how bad he's hurtin'."

They led the horses down the street and tied them at the hitch rack in front of a cafe. Casebolt complained all the time they were inside, but Hank noticed that he managed to put away two stacks of flapjacks, a good-sized mound of bacon, and three cups of coffee.

Several other Rangers came into the place while Hank and Casebolt were eating. Hank nodded greetings to them. The organization seemed to be full of good men, which came as no surprise to Hank. He had heard plenty about the previous band of Rangers from his father, and from the looks of things, this new bunch was much the same—cool under fire, seasoned veterans despite the relative youth of many of them. And scattered through the ranks were old-timers like Casebolt, of course, men who had seen and done it all and who were largely responsible for the state being as settled as it was. There was still plenty of work for all of them to do, however, and Hank just hoped he was up to the task. He wanted to make sure he deserved to wear that silver star on a silver circle.

If the events of the day before were any indication, though, it was going to be bloody work. And maybe that was all he was good for.

Hank sipped his coffee and tried not to think about that. He had slept well enough, not haunted by any dreams about Doyle Kimbrough's death. But he had not forgotten what had happened. It had all gone too quickly to feel any fear at the time, but Hank knew that it could just as easily have been him and Casebolt lying dead there beside the San Gabriel River.

"Well, you about ready to go?" Casebolt asked after he had drained the last of his coffee.

"I suppose so," Hank said. He pushed back his chair and stood up, lifting his hat from the table and settling it on his head.

As they mounted up, Casebolt said, "I want to ride down by the river and see if I can find me some moss for this tooth."

"What good's that going to do?"

"My daddy always said chewin' moss was the best thing in the world you can do for a toothache. Reckon it's time I found out if he was right."

They had to cross the river anyway to reach the road to San Antonio, so Hank didn't mind stopping for a few minutes while Casebolt hunted up some moss on the side of a tree. The older Ranger wadded up the green growth into a ball and put in into his mouth. Chewing down on it, he made a face for a moment, then began to nod.

"I think it's gettin' better!" he said excitedly. "Damned if it ain't!"

"That's good," Hank said, sitting easily in his saddle on the banks of the Colorado. "Reckon you should gather some to take with you?"

"Shoot, it won't be no trouble to find more moss 'tween here and San Antone." Casebolt swung back up into the saddle. He grinned as he chewed. "Lordy, it sure feels good not to be hurtin' no more."

Hank had his doubts about the curative powers of moss, but he kept his mouth shut as he and Casebolt put their horses down the road to San Antonio.

As Hank had expected, his partner's tooth was hurting again before they reached San Marcos. Casebolt started casting back in his memory for other remedies he had heard of. "Be on the lookout for an ant bed," he told Hank. "Seems I recollect somebody tellin' me that if you put a red ant on a bad tooth, it'll sting the nerve and kill it."

"Sure," Hank agreed. "Don't you reckon it'd be liable to sting other places inside your mouth, too?"

"They never said nothin' about that."

They made camp that night between San Marcos and New Braunfels, having covered thirty-some-odd miles from Austin. They were making good time, Hank thought, and would probably reach San Antonio late the next day.

Their route still led between the hill country to the west and the farm land to the east, and this area between the two was a pretty place, full of rolling, timbered hills and clear, cool streams.

The two Rangers rode through the German-settled community of New Braunfels about midday, and Casebolt wasn't just about to pass up the opportunity to stop for a meal. "These folks make the best sausage you'll ever eat, son," he told Hank. "I got to stop at a store and get me some oil of cloves for this tooth, too."

28

Casebolt was right about the sausage. Hank enjoyed the meal they had at a small, steep-roofed *Gasthaus*. He even liked the black bread, the likes of which he had never before tasted. The girl who brought them their food was young and blond and buxom, and her smile brought warmth to Hank's face. Under other circumstances, he decided, he wouldn't have minded staying in New Braunfels for a while.

Hank had heard folks talking about San Antone all his life, but he was not prepared for the size of the place, extending as it did for great distances out over the plains. Hank and Casebolt reached outlying communities of red-roofed adobe houses long before they came into sight of the main part of town. And every couple of miles, it seemed, they passed a mission or a church. The stone missions, many of them surrounded by gardens full of brightly colored flowers, seemed to give off an air of antiquity. According to Casebolt, most of them had been there a hundred and fifty years or so, unchanged by the town that had grown up around them.

Everywhere he looked, Hank saw the brown faces of Mexicans, reminding him of his journey to El Paso more than a decade earlier. Their laughter and the liquid rippling of their language filled the air. That brought back memories, too, as did the sight of an adobe cantina with men relaxing in the shade of a tree in front of it, passing around a bottle of tequila. Hank and the big man called Buffalo Newcomb had visited more than one cantina just like that on their journey through West Texas. He would not have survived that trip if it had not been for the massive, bearded Indian fighter and wanderer.

Hank wondered, not for the first time, what had happened to Buffalo since the last time he had seen him, a long, long time ago . . .

The sun was setting, and it was unlikely that he and Casebolt would be able to get started on their search for the Whitaker gang tonight. But they ought to let the local authorities know they had arrived, Hank thought, and said as much.

"Reckon we could go see the sheriff," the older Ranger agreed. The oil of cloves he had bought in New Braunfels had soothed the pain in his jaw to a certain extent, and he was in a better mood again. "Them great seizers always like to know when some other lawman's in their bailiwick."

They rode downtown, passing another old mission. Unlike the others they had seen, this one was in a state of disrepair, except for an area that was being used as a grain warehouse. Casebolt reined in, an uncommonly solemn look on his grizzled face. Nodding toward the mission, he said, "That there's the Alamo, Hank. Don't reckon there'd be any Texas Rangers or even a State of Texas without what happened there."

Hank looked at the ramshackle old mission in the gathering dusk. It didn't look impressive, but he had heard enough stories about the famous battle between the die-hard Texicans and Santa Anna's army to understand the significance of the place. Liberty and freedom in Texas had been born here, and it was a damn shame that the mission had gotten so run-down. That was progress for you, he supposed. There wasn't much time for the past when a man was busy carving out the future.

"I won't never forget how I felt when the word came about what happened at the Alamo and at Goliad," Casebolt went on, his voice hollow with memory. "My family had pretty much stayed out of the fightin', but when we heard what Santa Anna had done, my daddy and my brothers and me all got on our hosses and went lookin' for Sam Houston. We found the army in time to get joined up for San Jacinto. Won't never forget that day, neither."

Hank nodded, caught up in the older man's musings. He had heard similar stories from his grandfather, and he was impressed once again with the special breed of people it had taken to come here and settle this land.

The two Rangers rode on, Hank casting a glance back over his shoulder at the Alamo.

Night fell rapidly, but the street was lit almost as bright as day by the illumination that came from saloons and cantinas. There was still plenty of laughter in the air, along with music from pianos and guitars. Casebolt looked longingly at some of the places they passed, but they rode on to the Bexar County courthouse, where they found a young deputy on duty in the sheriff's office.

The deputy looked to be barely out of his teens, and his eyes widened as the two men in range clothes strode into the office. He stared for a moment at the Ranger badges, obviously impressed, then finally said, "Howdy. What can I do for you?"

"We're lookin' for the sheriff," Casebolt replied.

The youngster said, "You can probably find him over at the Longhorn. It's just down the street. Say, you're the Rangers Sheriff Buell sent for, aren't you?''

"That's right, son."

"Well, you got here just in time. Folks are real upset about that Whitaker owlhoot. He and his gang hit a train just south of here a couple of days ago. Made quite a haul, and they killed the express messenger, to boot.''

Hank frowned and exchanged a glance with Casebolt. The news didn't surprise Hank, remembering Whitaker as he did.

"You're here to track down Whitaker, aren't you?" the deputy was saying.

"That's our job, all right," Casebolt admitted. "You say Buell's probably over at the Longhorn?"

"Right. I don't guess it's any secret that the sheriff likes to take a drink of an evening.''

Casebolt grinned. "He ain't the only one, sonny. Come on, Hank.''

They left their horses tied in front of the courthouse and walked down the street to the Longhorn Saloon, a huge establishment that took up a whole city block. The place had entrances on two sides, both of which sported a massive spread of horns above the batwings, decorations that gave the place its name. Inside, it was a typical frontier saloon, maybe a little higher class than most. There was a dance floor, plenty of tables for both drinking and gambling, and a long, L-shaped bar backed by glittering mirrors. Hank and Casebolt pushed through the batwings and into a wall of noise and smoke.

They made their way across the crowded floor, their badges drawing a few surprised, worried looks from some of the customers who were probably wanted on some charge or other. The attitude of the two new-comers made it plain that they weren't here to arrest anyone, though. The noise in the saloon had dropped off a little when they first entered, but it was back up to its previous level by the time they reached the bar.

"Couple of beers," Casebolt said to the white-aproned bartender who came up to take their order. The man's hair was slicked down and he wore sleeve gaiters. Without the apron he would have looked more like a gambler than a bardog, Hank thought. After the man had drawn their beers and placed the foaming mugs in front of them, Casebolt went on, "We're lookin' for Sheriff Buell."

The bartender nodded toward the elbow where the bar made its right-angle turn. "He's down there talking to the boss," the man said. "There's not going to be any trouble, is there?"

Casebolt frowned. "Why should there be?"

The bartender shrugged and turned away without answering.

Hank and Casebolt picked up their beers and strolled down the length of the bar toward the two men the bartender had indicated. One of them was a chunky, solid-looking man in a rumpled black suit and a battered Stetson. There was a Remington holstered on his hip underneath his coat and a badge pinned to his vest. He had bushy eyebrows and a heavy black moustache, and Hank suspected he was Sheriff Buell.

The other man wore a suit as well, but his was clean and pressed and much more expensive than the sheriff's. He had gray hair and a freshly shaven face, and he smelled faintly of bay rum. No doubt this man was the owner of the Longhorn.

"How long have I been coming in here, Nate?" Buell was asking as Hank and Casebolt came up.

"A long time, Sheriff. I know that," the saloonkeeper replied.

"Has there ever been any trouble in that time? Some that I started instead of finishing for somebody else, I mean?"

The other man shook his head. "You've never started a fight, Sheriff. I know that."

"Then why start worrying now about some two-bit gunny?" Buell demanded. "If he comes in here looking for me, I'll just arrest him and throw his butt in my jail."

Casebolt spoke up. "I don't reckon it's that Whitaker feller you're talkin' about, is it, Sheriff?"

Buell turned and saw the two Rangers, and his lined face broke into a broad grin that just as quickly vanished. "So you two jaspers finally got here, did you?" he growled. "It's about time. Whitaker pulled another robbery day before yesterday. Folks around here are howling for my head."

"Well, we'll do what we can to keep 'em from gettin' it," Casebolt replied. "And you didn't answer my question, Sheriff."

The local lawman reached up and rubbed a hand over his weary face. "No, I wasn't talking about Whitaker," he said. "I've been out looking for that bastard for two days now, and tonight when I got back to town,

I found out somebody's been looking for me. The brother of some kid I sent to prison a while back figures he's got a score to settle."

The saloonkeeper waved a hand at the mirrors behind the bar. "You can see why I don't want a lot of gunplay in here, Sheriff."

"All right, dammit," Buell grumbled. "Let me finish this watered-down stuff you call whiskey, and I'll get out of here." He picked up a glass from the bar and tossed down the amber liquid in it.

As he did so, someone near the side-street entrance of the saloon let out a yell. A table overturned as several of the customers leaped for cover. Hank jerked his head around to see what was causing the commotion. A man carrying a shotgun had just stepped into the saloon.

"Buell!" he shouted hoarsely. "Show yourself, you son-of-a-bitch."

The sheriff plunked the empty whiskey glass down on the bar and turned to face the shotgun-wielding stranger. In a voice that carried through the sudden quiet in the place, he said calmly, "I'm right here, mister."

The man wheeled around toward him, and the menacing barrels of the scattergun made more of the Longhorn's patrons scurry out of the line of fire. The muzzles of the shotgun stopped when they were lined up on Buell, and the man carrying the gun said, "So there you are! You been hidin' from me all day, but I knew you couldn't hide forever."

"I haven't been hiding from anybody," Buell said. "I've been out trying to do my job, just like I was when I arrested your brother, Knepper."

"Danny was just a kid!"

"It don't matter how old he was when he broke the law. He was old enough to rob that hardware store and pistol-whip the owner," Buell pointed out. "Now why don't you put that greener away and go home, 'fore you get into trouble yourself?"

The man shook his head. He was a big-boned man with a shock of yellow hair. His clothes were those of a cowhand, but the gun he wore said he was more than a simple cow nurse—or at least he fancied himself more than that. But as Hank stood very still and watched the man, he couldn't help but draw some conclusions from the fact that Knepper was facing the sheriff with a shotgun, rather than relying on his six-shooter. The man might think of himself as a gunfighter, but he seemed to be admitting he had some limitations. It might be possible to reason with him.

Hank glanced over at Casebolt. The older Ranger hadn't moved; he was standing next to the bar, the mug of beer in his hand. On the other side of Sheriff Buell, the saloonkeeper had edged away, putting some distance between himself and the lawman. Hank was standing beside Casebolt, the older man between himself and the bar.

He took a step toward Knepper, still staying out of the man's direct line of fire. At this range, though, and with a shotgun, that didn't matter much. If Knepper started blasting, odds were Hank and Casebolt would both catch some buckshot. Hank said, "Hold on a minute, fella."

Buell grated, "Dammit, kid, don't get in the way!"

Hank kept his eyes on Knepper as he said, "Sorry, Sheriff. I just thought this man ought to know that there are a couple of Texas Rangers here."

Knepper licked his lips. "Rangers?" he rasped. For the first time, he noticed the badges that Hank and Casebolt wore. He had been too caught up in his desire for vengeance to take note of them earlier.

"That's right," Hank said, keeping his voice cool, remembering how he had seen his grandfather talk angry men out of doing stupid things. "If you start shooting in here, it'll be our duty to help Sheriff Buell arrest you."

Hank kept edging forward as he talked. He knew without looking behind him that Casebolt was moving off to the side, away from Buell. The three lawmen were forming a triangle, with Hank as its leading point. Already, there was probably enough distance between them that Knepper couldn't down all three of them. At least one man would be left standing.

And that man would kill Knepper, sure as anything.

Knepper's eyes flicked from side to side as he tried to keep up with what was happening. He had somehow lost control of the situation and he knew it.

Hank was equally aware that he was in the most dangerous position. If Knepper turned the greener on him, there was a good chance he would be blown in half. Quietly, Hank went on, "Now, you can't go around waving guns and threatening folks, but if you put down that shotgun and come along quiet-like, I don't imagine you'll have to do anything except pay a fine and spend a few nights in jail. If you start shooting, it'll be a lot worse."

There were beads of sweat on Knepper's forehead now, and the saloon was so quiet that his harsh breathing was clearly audible. After a moment, he said, "But Buell put my kid brother in jail. God knows what's going to happen to him there."

"Maybe he'll serve his time and come home," Hank pointed out. "You'd want to be there when he does, wouldn't you?"

"Well, sure—"

"Not stuck in a grave with a cheap wooden marker," Hank said quickly, boring in now that all Knepper's doubts and fears were surfacing. He held out his empty right hand. The left still held a mug of beer. "Give me the shotgun."

Knepper let the twin barrels drop toward the floor as he took a deep breath. He stepped closer to Hank and took his finger out of the trigger guard, then awkwardly thrust the weapon at Hank with his left hand. "Take it," he said.

Hank reached out, his fingers closing over the breech of the weapon just as Casebolt yelled, "Hank! No!"

Knepper's right hand dipped toward his holstered pistol. Both of Hank's hands were full now, and he knew he couldn't drop either the shotgun or the mug and still hope to beat the man to the draw. Knepper had moved forward so that Hank was between him and Casebolt and Buell, shielding him from the lawmen.

Even before his thoughts were complete, Hank's instincts had taken over. His left wrist flicked the beer into Knepper's face as he lunged at the man. Shoving the shotgun ahead of him, he slammed it across Knepper's midsection, then whipped the mug across his face with the other hand. Grunting in pain and blinking his eyes against the sting of the beer, Knepper still managed to get his gun out.

Hank had slowed the man down enough so that he was able to get out of the way, though. He flung himself to the side as several guns crashed, the reports blending together into one sustained roar. Rolling on the sawdust-covered floor as he landed, Hank came up with his own pistol in his hand. In the same moment he saw that it wouldn't be needed. Knepper had been thrown backward by two slugs, one hitting each side of his chest. He was sprawled on the floor, his gun fallen beside him, his shirt bloody and his eyes glassy in an unseeing gaze toward the ceiling of the barroom.

Casebolt holstered his gun, but Buell kept his ready until he had stalked forward and prodded the body enough to be convinced that Knepper was dead. Hank put his gun away and came over to Casebolt's side. He grimaced as he glanced at the dead gunman.

"Reckon I fell for an old trick," he said somewhat sheepishly.

Casebolt rasped a hand along his lean jaw, on the side away from the sore tooth. "Well, you're young yet," he said. "You live long enough, you'll get so's you won't be fooled so easy."

"You knew I wasn't talking him out of it for a second, didn't you?"

Buell rejoined them at that moment and said, "Reckon we both did. Knepper came in here to kill somebody, namely me, and he wasn't going to leave until he did just that. But you had no way of knowing how crazy that ol' boy was."

The saloonkeeper was fingering a fresh bullet hole in the bar, about halfway down, right between where Casebolt and Buell had been standing. Knepper had done pretty good, Hank thought, to get a shot off that had gone in the right general direction.

"I'll send somebody over to fetch him to the undertaker's," Buell told the saloonkeeper. Turning to Hank and Casebolt, he went on, "Why don't you two come on over to the office with me? I'll tell you what I know about Isom Whitaker. It's not much, but maybe it'll help."

"Thanks, Sheriff," Casebolt replied, then paused as he started toward the door of the saloon. "Say, you ain't got nobody else gunnin' for you, have you?"

"Not right now," Buell answered with a laugh.

"All right, we'll go with you, then." Another thought occurred to the veteran Ranger. "You don't happen to have a good dentist in this town, do you?"

Chapter Five

"Been around the hill country much?" Casebolt asked Hank the next day as they rode northwest out of San Antonio.

"Not at all," Hank replied. They had left town less than an hour earlier, and he could already tell that the terrain was getting considerably rougher. There were more gullies, and their banks were steeper, the dry stream beds at the bottom of them rockier. The brush was thicker, too, and it clawed at horse and rider both as they followed the sometimes narrow trail.

"Mighty pretty country," Casebolt said as he swayed in the saddle. "Reckon you'll like it."

"I might like it better if we weren't hunting for Isom Whitaker in it," Hank said dryly.

Sheriff Marcus Buell didn't know much about Isom Whitaker except that the former State Policeman and his gang had been making life hell for him these past few weeks. Buell was a proud man; it had not been easy for him to call in the Rangers to help. But Whitaker had pulled off so many successful robberies and slipped away so many times that something had to be done. Requesting the help of the newly re-formed

Rangers would at least divert some of the blame from the sheriff's head.

Following the train holdup a couple of days earlier, Buell and a hastily formed posse had pursued the gang northwest away from San Antonio. They had never caught up to Whitaker and his men, though, and the outlaws had eventually disappeared into the rugged landscape. Buell had spent most of two days combing that part of Bexar County for any sign of them, with no luck.

"I think they've left this part of the country," Buell had told the two Rangers in his office the night before. "Maybe that's just wishful thinking on my part, but I really figure they've holed up somewhere over in the hills. There're a hell of a lot of places to hide between here and West Texas."

That was true enough. As he and Casebolt left Bexar County and crossed over into Bandera County, Hank thought that half the outlaw gangs in the state could be hiding here and have room left over.

That morning, they had ridden down to the spot where Whitaker and his men had hit the train. Buell had accompanied them and pointed out where the blasting powder had been used to blow up the tracks. He waved a hand toward the northwest and said, "We chased 'em for half a day but never got close enough to throw lead at them."

"What's in that direction?" Hank had asked.

"Lots of hills, some ranches, the Medina River. Town called Bandera is the first good-sized settlement up the Medina Valley. From there Whitaker could head for Kerrsville or Junction, just depends on which way he wanted to go. Or he could still be somewhere around Bandera. There's just no way of knowing."

"There's one way," Casebolt had grunted. "Go up there and root him out."

It was a simple enough plan. It was also the only one they had.

At mid-morning, they struck the Medina River. It was a winding stream lined with large trees—cypress, cottonwood, elm, and live oak. At times it meandered through broad, low-lying valleys, at others it cut through the rugged hills. Hank and Casebolt followed the river whenever they could. When they couldn't, they rode on the rocky ridges above the stream. It would take them to Bandera sooner or later, and they had already decided that the town would make a good starting point for their search.

They passed a few farms and ranches, stopping to ask if the families who had settled here had seen any sign of Whitaker's men. At first the people were cautious, the women and children usually hiding inside the cabins while the men came out to greet the visitors. Most of the men carried rifles and seemed to be ready to use them. But once they saw the Ranger badges, everything changed.

Hank and Casebolt could have eaten a dozen meals on their way to Bandera if they had accepted all the invitations they received. They were less successful at finding out anything about Whitaker, though. No one had seen him.

That afternoon, as they were nearing the town, Casebolt pulled his horse to a stop on a high ridge that was dotted with cedars. The Medina River was to the south, and to the north the hills rolled away as far as the eye could see.

Two remarkably similar peaks jutted up far in the distance to the northeast. Casebolt nodded toward them. "Reckon those must be the Twin Sisters," he said. "Been a long time since I've seen 'em from this side. Used to use 'em as a landmark on the trail between San Antone and Fredericksburg, back when I was drivin' a freight wagon." He pointed more to the north and asked, "See that gap in the hills?"

Hank looked where he was indicating and saw the notch. From the looks of it, it would be the only good way through the range of hills that marked the northern boundary of the Medina Valley. "I see it," Hank said.

"That's Bandera Pass," Casebolt told him. "I heard Cap'n Jack Hays tell many a time 'bout the fight him and a bunch of Rangers had there with the Comanch'. Killed over a hundred of the savages, they did, includin' the chief." Casebolt shook his head. "Damn, I wish I'd been there. Things just ain't been the same since most of the Indians went up to the Panhandle to do their fightin'."

Hank chuckled at the longing in the older man's voice. "Anyway," Casebolt went on after a moment, "just on the other side of the pass is Camp Verde."

Hank nodded. "I've heard of that. That's where they had the camels, wasn't it?"

"Damn right. Ugliest lookin' critters you'd ever want to see. Me and some other fellers rode in there back in '56, and there they were, big as life and twice as nasty. They was the spittin'est, bitin'est varmints I ever saw, I tell you that for sure. That just goes to show you what kind of damn fool ideas the army can get ever' now and then. I hear tell there's still some of them beasts roamin' around in the hills, but I don't set much store by that. It's been nigh onto eight years since the post was closed down. I reckon any of them camels that were runnin' wild are all dead by now."

"Maybe so," Hank said, thinking of the stories he had heard about the bizarre animals. It was said they could carry almost as much freight as a wagon and could travel over rougher terrain than any mule. Hank patted his mount's neck and grinned. He was glad folks today were still riding horses and not camels.

The two Rangers pushed on, and in late afternoon they followed the river into the town of Bandera. The trail widened out into a decent road that became the town's main street. The road crossed the river, which made a north-south jog here before continuing on its generally easterly course, on an old wooden bridge. Just beyond the river on the right was a large building made of limestone, and a sign on it announced that it was the Schmidtke and Hay Store. The rest of the town spread out to the south of the road, except for a few houses scattered on a wooded slope to the north.

Hank and Casebolt drew rein in front of the store just as two men emerged from its doorway carrying boxes of supplies. The men placed the provisions on the bed of a mule-drawn wagon parked in front of the building, then one of the men climbed to the driver's seat. He flicked the reins to get the four mules in the team moving, turning as he did so to call, "So long, George. Thanks again."

The man on the porch of the store nodded. "Be seeing you, Amasa," he replied. He was a well-built man wearing a canvas apron. The sleeves of his shirt were rolled up to reveal brawny forearms. The man was balding, but he had a full, dark moustache. Turning to Hank and Casebolt, he nodded and went on, "Howdy, gents. Something I can do for you?"

"Name's Casebolt," the older Ranger said, resting his hands on the pommel of his saddle and leaning forward to ease his back. "This here's Hank Littleton. We're lookin' for the sheriff."

The storekeeper nodded, his eyes on their badges. "Rangers, eh? You here on business?"

"That's right."

The man stepped forward and reached up to shake Casebolt's hand. "My name is George Hay," he said. "Anything you need while you're in town, you come to see me. As for the sheriff, you'll probably find him at the county offices. They're down the street, next to the jail."

"And where'll we find the jail?" Casebolt asked.

A grin stretched over George Hay's face. "Oh, you can't miss it," he told them. "If Sam Knight's not in his office, reckon he's gone home for the day. His house is a block south of the jail, on Eleventh Street."

Casebolt nodded. "Much obliged." He turned his horse away from the building and started on down the street, Hank riding beside him.

Hank looked around Bandera as they rode. It was a pleasant enough place, he thought. It reminded him a little of San Saba. They passed another mercantile, this one belonging to the Huffmeyer Brothers. There were all the usual establishments of a small town like this one—a saddle maker, a gunsmith, an apothecary, a carpenter shop, and several saloons. The steeples of a couple of churches were visible on side streets south of the main avenue. There were quite a few wagons parked on the street, and people who were standing on the porches of the various businesses cast curious glances at the two strangers.

Casebolt muttered, more to himself than Hank, "Sam Knight . . . Somethin' familiar about that name."

"I just hope he doesn't mind the Rangers coming into his territory," Hank commented.

Casebolt shook his head. "Don't reckon he will. He probably don't want Isom Whitaker hangin' around here any more than Buell wanted him in San Antone."

Up ahead, on the left side of the road, they suddenly spotted an unusual building. It was about fourteen feet square, made of what appeared to be thick cypress timbers. Hank had never seen such a solid-looking frame building. That solidness was emphasized by the fact that there was only one window in the place; that single opening was small and high, almost on a level with the flat roof. A ladder was propped against the building on one side. There was no door in front.

He reined in and said, "What kind of a place is that?"

Casebolt grinned. "Reckon that's the hoosegow Mr. Hay was tellin' us about. There's probably a trapdoor in the roof, and that'll be the only way in or out. Not a bad idea for keepin' prisoners." He nodded toward the whitewashed frame building next to the jail. "And that's probably the county offices. Come on."

They rode up to the building next to the jail and tied their horses at the hitch rack in front of it. Their footsteps echoed hollowly as they climbed onto the wide planks of the porch. Casebolt tried the door and found it unlocked.

They stepped into a hallway that was growing dark with the oncoming dusk. Someone had already lit a lamp in one of the rooms to the left of the corridor. Its warm yellow glow drew them to the doorway.

The room was small, and a big roll-top desk took up most of the space. On top of the desk sat the lantern that was giving off the light. A lot of papers were spread out on the desk—mostly reward dodgers, Hank saw with a quick glance—and the man sitting in the chair in front of the desk had probably been studying them before he dozed off.

His head jerked up at the sound of booted feet in the hallway, and his hand went toward the gun on his hip. He stopped the gesture and blinked as he saw that the newcomers meant him no harm. He straightened in the chair, nodded to them, said, "Evening. Come on in."

Hank and Casebolt stepped into the office. The man at the desk spotted their badges and stood up quickly, thrusting his hand out to them.

"Sorry, fellas, didn't realize you were Rangers at first," he said. "I'm Sam Knight."

Casebolt shook his hand. "You the sheriff hereabouts?"

"For all of Bandera County," Knight grinned. He shook hands with Hank, then lifted his other hand to rub at his eyes for a second. "Reckon I must've nodded off. Haven't been sleeping too good at night lately. Well, come in and make yourselves at home, Rangers."

"This's Hank Littleton, and I'm Joe Casebolt. Just wanted to let you know we were in town, Sheriff."

Knight sat down again, waving his visitors into a pair of ladderback chairs that sat against the wall. He said, "You boys here on business, or just passing through?"

"Business," Casebolt said. "We're lookin' for a feller name of Isom Whitaker. 'Case you ain't heard of him, he's an owlhoot, and him and his gang been robbin' trains and stages down around San Antone. Killed a few people, too."

Knight nodded. He was a thick-bodied man in his forties, clean shaven, and just a little too battered to be called handsome. He had thick black hair that was touched in quite a few places with silver. "I've heard of Whitaker," he said. "Think I've got a poster on him here somewhere. You don't think he's somewhere around Bandera, do you?"

"Could be. He held up a train a few days back and then lit out in this direction."

Hank remained silent, content for the moment to let Casebolt do the talking. The other Ranger was older and more experienced and had dealt with local lawmen like this before. Despite the fact that he had been dozing when they came in, Knight struck Hank as probably a competent officer, and he didn't seem bothered by the fact that Rangers had entered his jurisdiction.

Knight was shaking his head. "I don't figure I'd recognize this Whitaker fella if I was to see him, but I know we haven't had any trouble around here lately."

"I don't reckon you would have . . . yet," Casebolt replied. "Whitaker and his bunch was on the run, like I said, so chances are they'll be layin' low for a while. Sooner or later, they'll come out to pull another job."

The sheriff leaned forward in his chair and clasped his hands together in front of him. Hank saw that Knight's fingers were long and calloused and his knuckles were bony. They were the hands of a man who had worked hard his entire life.

"What can I do to help you?" Knight asked.

"You know this country hereabouts, don't you?"

"Reckon I do. I haven't lived here all my life, like some of the folks around here, but I've been sheriff long enough to poke around in most of the county."

"Then maybe you can tell us some places an outlaw like Whitaker might be liable to use for a hide-out," Casebolt said. "I figure we'll use the town here as our headquarters for a few days whilst we look around."

"All right," Knight agreed. "I can talk to some of the old-timers, too, find out if they know about any hidey-holes I don't."

"We'd be obliged." Casebolt stood up. "I reckon the next thing we need to do tonight is find a place to stay, for us and our hosses both."

Knight got to his feet, as did Hank. The sheriff said, "Colonel Duffy would be glad to put you up down at the Riverside Inn. It's just across the road from Huffmeyers', and there's a stable out back for your horses."

Hank remembered seeing the hotel as they rode into town. It was a large structure, built of cypress timbers, like most of the other buildings in town that weren't made of limestone.

As the men started toward the door of Sam Knight's office, Hank spoke for the first time. "You don't happen to have a dentist in town, do you?" he asked the sheriff.

Casebolt shot him an angry look. Back in San Antonio, he had backed out of going to the dentist Sheriff Buell had recommended, and during the ride up the Medina River today, had claimed that his sore tooth was much better. Hank had seen him flinch from time to time and rub at his jaw, though. The tooth had to still be bothering him.

Knight smiled at Hank. "You have a toothache, son?"

Hank shook his head and jerked a thumb at the glowering Casebolt. "Joe here is the one with the bad tooth."

"Dammit, I told you it was better!" Casebolt protested, but grimaced as he did so.

Knight grinned. "I was thinking about asking you fellas to come on over to my house for supper, but now I know I'm going to. My wife sets the best table in town, if I do say so myself, and she's got some lemon extract that'll fix that tooth right up."

"You reckon so?" Casebolt sounded anxious to believe Knight's claim.

"I'm sure of it." Knight snagged a Stetson from a nail in the wall next to the office door and settled it on his head, then slapped each of the Rangers on the back. "Come on, fellas. You're going home with me."

Chapter Six

The sun had dropped behind the hills as Sheriff Sam Knight led Hank and Casebolt from the small building that housed the Bandera County offices.

"Hope your missus won't be too put out, you showin' up with strangers for supper this way," Casebolt commented.

"Don't reckon you need to worry about that," Knight replied. "Faye's the best cook in these parts, and there's nothing she likes better than the chance to prove it. I hope you boys have a good appetite."

"You ever see a youngster that didn't?" Casebolt asked, grinning at Hank.

"Now, you can hold your own, Joe," Hank said, chuckling.

It took only a few moments to reach the sheriff's house. Tall trees threw the front yard into shadow, but lamplight glowed warmly through windows that were covered with lace curtains. The house was a single-story structure made of rough-hewn planks, which were made to look smoother with a good coat of whitewash. There was a covered verandah on the front of the house, and a small barn stood to its right. All in all, it reminded Hank a bit of his grandfather's house, with the same solid warmth about it.

"You can put your mounts in the barn or just tie them up here in the yard," Knight said. "There's plenty of grass for them to graze on."

Hank reached out for the reins of Casebolt's horse and said, "Thanks, Sheriff." He tied the animals to trees about ten feet apart.

There were two shallow steps leading up to the verandah. Knight took them in one stride, looking over his shoulder to say, "Come on in and make yourselves comfortable. I'll let the womenfolk know you're here."

Hank wondered how many women were here. Knight's wife was the only one he had mentioned. With Casebolt at his side, Hank stepped up onto the long porch and went to the door that Knight had opened. The sheriff stood back to let the two visitors go in first.

Hank stepped into the house and stopped short. The prettiest girl he had seen in a long time was standing across the room, staring at him in surprise.

She had long brown hair that had been lightened by the sun until it was the color of milk with some molasses stirred into it. Her face was tanned, and while her features were not what could be considered beautiful, they were certainly appealing. Intelligent blue eyes looked keenly at Hank, becoming more curious as the surprise faded from them. She was slender and wore a homespun dress that looked good on her.

Casebolt bumped into Hank from behind and grunted, "What the hell . . . ?" Spotting the girl standing on the other side of the room, he immediately became flustered and grabbed for his hat. Sweeping it off, he went on hurriedly, "Beg pardon, missy."

Hank quickly took his own hat off. "Excuse us, ma'am."

The girl's lips curved into a smile. "That's quite all right," she said softly, her voice every bit as pretty as Hank would have expected it to be. "Won't you gentlemen come on in? Hello, Father."

Sam Knight had come through the front door after Casebolt. He grinned at the reactions of Hank and Casebolt and said, "Fellas, this is my daughter, Victoria. Victoria, these are a couple of Rangers who've come to pay us a visit here in Bandera. This is Joe Casebolt, and the young fella is . . ." He paused, obviously having forgotten Hank's name.

"Hank Littleton," he supplied. "We're pleased to meet you, Miss Knight."

"And I'm pleased to meet you, Mr. Littleton," Victoria Knight said. "You, too, Mr. Casebolt." She came forward and went up to Knight, raising herself on her toes to kiss his cheek. "I suppose I'd better go tell Mother that we have company for supper."

"Thanks, sweetheart." Knight patted his daughter's shoulder as she turned to leave the room, then he nodded toward chairs. "Have a seat and make yourselves at home." He unbuckled the gunbelt from around his waist and hung it on a nail just inside the door, along with his hat.

They sat down, Hank and Casebolt dropping their hats on the floor beside their chairs, and now that Victoria Knight was gone, Hank had a chance to look around the room. There was a large stone fireplace on one wall, cold now, of course. On the opposite wall was a long, heavy sofa; in front of it on the floor was a buffalo rug. He and Casebolt were sitting in brocaded armchairs, while Knight had settled down in a massive rocking chair with ornate carving on its arms. The chair had plenty of nicks and scratches on it, and several places were worn smooth. Hank saw that Knight's hands fell naturally on those smooth places and knew that this was the sheriff's special chair. It had probably been in the family for decades.

On hooks over the fireplace hung a Kentucky long rifle, a powderhorn and shot bag with it. Another piece of family history, Hank supposed. In the rear half of the room was a long table where the family took its meals. Beyond that was the door that led to the kitchen. A china cabinet sat on one side of the door, and on the other was a bookshelf filled with leather-bound volumes.

Compared with the Ranger barracks and saloons and stables and train stations and cheap cafes where Hank had spent most of his time in recent months, Sam Knight's house was the most pleasant place Hank had seen. A part of him felt almost like he was returning home.

No place he had ever lived had possessed such a strong female presence, though. The curtains on the windows, the china cabinet, the needlework placed on one arm of the sofa to be picked up later, the lithographs of pastoral scenes on the walls—all these things said that women of beauty and grace lived here.

A moment later, when the sheriff's wife, Faye, emerged from the kitchen, he could see where Victoria had gotten her good looks. The older woman had the same striking features as her daughter. Her hair, worn in a bun, was the same shade as Victoria's except where the years had lightly touched it with gray. She wore an apron over a print dress and wiped her hands on it as she smiled at the visitors. "Good evening, gentlemen," she said. "I hope you like fried chicken and potatoes and greens, with plenty of gravy and biscuits, and apple pie."

Hank and Casebolt stood up to greet her, and the older Ranger's face lit up as she spoke. "Ma'am, you sure do know how to make a feller feel welcome," he said fervently. "I ain't had a good home-cooked meal like that in I don't know when."

Knight said, "Faye, Ranger Casebolt here has a bad tooth. You think you could fix him up after supper?"

"Why, certainly," she replied with a smile. "Are you in a great deal of pain, Mr. Casebolt?"

He put a hand up to his jaw and tried to look strong. "It hurts right smart, ma'am," he said, "but I reckon it's tolerable."

"Are you sure you'll be up to eating?" Faye asked anxiously. "I wouldn't want to cause you any extra pain."

"Oh, no, ma'am, it'll be fine," Casebolt said quickly, distressed at the thought of missing the meal.

"Well, after we've eaten, I'll put some lemon extract on the bad tooth for you. That always does the trick."

"Yes, ma'am. We really appreciate you feedin' us like this, without no warnin', I mean."

"It's no problem, Mr. Casebolt. I always prepare plenty. A sheriff's wife gets used to unexpected visitors, isn't that right, Sam?"

"We've had our share," Knight chuckled.

The smells coming from the kitchen were mouth watering, and at that moment, Victoria came back into the room carrying a platter of fried chicken. As she placed it on the table, her mother said, "Excuse me."

Over the next couple of minutes, the two women brought several more dishes from the kitchen to the table. The growling of Hank's stomach reminded him of how long it had been since he and Casebolt had stopped for lunch at a settler's cabin. Knight stood up from his rocking chair and went to the table, motioning for Hank and Casebolt to join him and sit to his right.

Victoria filled a plate for her father while her mother did likewise for the Rangers. Then the two women helped themselves and sat down, Faye at the other end of the table from her husband, Victoria across from Hank. As she settled down in her chair, Hank suddenly looked down at his plate, embarrassed for some reason. Maybe it was because of how pretty she was, he thought. Maybe it was the slightly mocking smile she gave him. . . .

Casebolt was reaching for his fork when Sam Knight said, "Would either of you gentlemen care to say grace?"

After a moment's hesitation, Casebolt said, "Seein' as it's your house, Sheriff, might be best if you did."

"Of course." Knight bowed his head, and the others followed suit. Even with his head down, though, Hank could still sense that Victoria was watching him out of slitted eyes. Her father went on, "Lord, we thank You for the blessings of family and food and visitors who we hope will become friends. Amen."

"Amen," the two women echoed softly.

Casebolt dug in then, acquitting himself well with the fried chicken and the mounds of potatoes and greens. If his tooth slowed him down any, Hank couldn't tell it.

Hank ate with enthusiasm, too. Knight's boast about his wife's cooking proved to be a plain and simple fact. There was little conversation around the table as they ate, everyone preferring to concentrate on the food.

When they were done, Victoria went back to the kitchen and brought out the deep-dish apple pie. Hank suppressed a groan, not sure that he had enough room left for the treat. He found some, though, enough for two helpings, in fact.

Casebolt looked happier than he had in days.

Finally, the meal was over and the women began to clear away the empty dishes and platters. Sam Knight stood up, stretched, and said, "How about a little brandy, fellas?"

"That don't sound half bad," Casebolt agreed.

The three men went back to the other half of the big room, taking their coffee cups with them. Hank and Casebolt sat down while Knight took a bottle from the mantel over the fireplace and uncorked it. He splashed the brandy into their cups and then took his own seat in the rocking chair. After sipping the liquor, he grinned at his guests and said, "What did I tell you about the wife's cooking?"

"Best meal I et in a long, long time," Casebolt agreed, settling back in his chair.

"Me, too," Hank said, glancing up as Victoria Knight came out of the kitchen to remove more of what was left on the table. "The very best."

She glanced up at him, and the little smile on her face warmed him up even more than the brandy.

Knight took a cigar from his vest pocket, scratched a lucifer into life on the sole of his boot, and lit it. Casebolt and Hank both shook their heads when he offered one to them. Hank was content to sit right where he was, sipping good brandy and basking in the contentment of a good meal in very enjoyable surroundings.

"Now, about this Whitaker fella . . ." Knight said, breaking the mood. Hank sat up straighter.

"Who?" The question came from Victoria, who had come back into the room without the three men noticing.

"Isom Whitaker, Miss Knight," Casebolt said. "He's the owlhoot we're chasin'."

"Oh." Victoria sounded vaguely disappointed. "I wasn't sure why you had come to Bandera."

Knight sighed. "I'm afraid my daughter isn't real fond of the law business," he said.

"I just don't like seeing people I care about risking their lives all the time," Victoria replied quickly. "Why, Mother and I never know when you leave in the morning if some desperado is going to come into town and . . . and shoot you, Father."

"That's not very likely in Bandera, darlin'," Knight said with a short laugh. "This place has gotten downright civilized."

"Maybe recently," Victoria said. "But it hasn't always been that way. What about—"

Knight shook his head, cutting her off abruptly. His features had suddenly become stern. "That's nothing that needs talked about now," he told her.

Trying not to sound as nervous as he felt, Hank turned to Victoria and said, "We didn't mean to upset you, ma'am. Maybe it'd be best if we went on down to the hotel—"

"No," Victoria said with a shake of her head. "I'm sorry. You men go on with your law talk. I'll stay where I belong." She turned on her heel and pushed through the door into the kitchen.

After a moment, Knight laughed and said, "I'm afraid my gal's got a mind of her own, gents, and she doesn't mind telling folks about it, either."

"Nothing wrong with that," Hank said.

Knight shrugged. He drained the last of his brandy, then leaned forward, his cigar held between two fingers. "You wanted to know where a fella like Whitaker might hide around here. Well, I can think of several places right off hand. There are creeks all over this county, not to mention the Medina itself and the Sabinal, and they've cut gullies all through the hills. The way they meander around and turn back on themselves, there are probably dozens of little canyons where folks could hide."

"That's what we figured," Casebolt said. "Where do you reckon we ought to start lookin'?"

For the next few minutes, Sam Knight gave them directions to a handful of likely spots that Whitaker might be using as a hide-out. Hank paid close attention, trying not to let his concentration stray when Victoria came back into the room and took one of the books from the shelves. She went to the sofa and sat down to open the volume and start reading. A few minutes later, her mother joined her and resumed the needlework she had laid aside earlier. Every so often, Hank's glance strayed over to them.

Captain McNelly would be damned disappointed in him, he told himself sternly, letting his mind wander like that just because there was a pretty girl in the room.

But then Captain McNelly had never seen Victoria Knight.

Finally, when the local lawman had given them all the hints he could about where to start looking, Casebolt nodded and said, "Much obliged for the help, Sheriff."

"Make it Sam, since you've set down to table with us."

"All right, Sam. Me 'n the boy'll start checkin' these places out first thing tomorrow. Happen we run onto Whitaker and his bunch, you reckon you could raise a posse to help us hogtie 'em?"

"I'm sure I can," Knight said. "There are plenty of men around here who've fought Indians and renegades both."

Casebolt picked up his hat and got to his feet, and Hank did likewise.

"We'll mosey on down to the hotel, then," Casebolt said. He turned to Faye and Victoria and went on, "Thanks again for the meal, ladies."

Faye stood up. "Wait just a moment, Mr. Casebolt. I never did attend to your tooth. Let me get that lemon extract." She hurried to the kitchen door and disappeared through it.

Hank turned his hat over in his hands and tried not to stare at Victoria Knight. He looked instead at the book she was reading and tried to make out the gilt lettering.

"It's a novel by Wilkie Collins, Mr. Littleton," Victoria said, taking Hank by surprise and embarrassing him again. "Have you read his work?"

Hank shook his head. "No, ma'am. We don't get much time for reading. Maybe a penny dreadful every now and then."

Victoria smiled. "This isn't much different, but it is rather exciting. Perhaps you'd like to borrow it if you're here in Bandera long enough."

"Yes, ma'am. That would be nice."

That was the last thing he wanted, Hank thought as he lied to her. On the other hand, he suddenly realized, if he did read the book, that would give him something to talk about with Victoria, instead of him having to stand around like some sort of lummox.

Faye came back into the room carrying a small bottle. She handed it to the older Ranger and said, "I'll let you take this with you, Mr. Casebolt. Put a drop or two on the sore tooth three times a day, and it should help."

"Thank you, ma'am. I'll do that," he promised. "Well, good night, ever'body."

Hank bid the family good night as well, then quickly left the room behind Casebolt. They untied their horses and swung up into the saddles. Riding away from the house and back toward Main Street, Casebolt grinned broadly in the moonlight and said, "If I didn't know better, Hank, I'd say you was sweet on that little gal."

"Well, then, you *don't* know any better," Hank responded flatly.

"Sure wish I knew how to read, so's I could borrer some books from her."

"I was just trying to be friendly. The sheriff was mighty nice to us."

"Yep, he was," Casebolt nodded. "Seems like a good feller. Reckon he'll invite us back to eat with 'em again?"

Hank shrugged. "I suppose he might."

"Well, then, I hope we don't find Whitaker for a while. A man could get right fond of Miz Knight's cookin'."

Hank couldn't resist getting a gibe of his own in. "Sounds to me like you're the one who's sweet on somebody, Joe. You'd better be careful; she's already married."

Casebolt snorted. "You don't know what you're talkin' about, boy. Come on, we'd best go on down to that hotel and get some sleep. We got outlaws to hunt in the mornin'."

Chapter Seven

There were several vacant rooms at the Riverside Inn. Hank and Casebolt rented a couple of adjoining ones on the second floor from Colonel Hugh Duffy, a handsome, sharp-eyed man who in addition to owning the town's best hotel was also a prominent local attorney.

They stabled their horses in the barn behind the hotel, then, carrying their warbags, went up to the second floor. Casebolt took the first room, tossing his bag on the bed and looking around critically. "Reckon it'll do," he said.

"Well, it's not as fancy as a blanket and a saddle and the open sky," Hank commented dryly.

Casebolt frowned. He took the little bottle of lemon extract from his pocket and placed it on a wooden dresser.

"Tooth bothering you again, Joe?" Hank asked. "You look a little perturbed."

Casebolt shook his head. "It ain't that. Ever since we left Knight's house, there's been somethin' botherin' me about him. I just can't figger out what it is."

"He seemed like a nice enough fella to me, and a good lawman, too,"

Hank said with a shrug. "He might've been dozing when we first went into his office, but you can't hold that against a man. I've seen you nod off in the saddle a time or two yourself."

"No, that ain't it. The longer we was around him, the more I felt like I had heard tell of him somewheres."

"Maybe it'll come back to you." Hank had to stifle a yawn. He shifted his warbag on his shoulder. "I'm going on to my room and get some sleep. We'll have plenty of riding to do tomorrow."

"That's right," Casebolt nodded. He waved a hand. "I ain't goin' to worry about it. Chances are it weren't too important anyhow."

"Good night, then."

"Night, Hank . . ."

Hank found the bed in his room softer than what he was used to and had some trouble falling asleep because of it, but weariness finally took over. Sleep claimed him, and so did dreams.

As Hank had predicted, the next day was a long one. He and Casebolt rode out after an early breakfast in the Riverside Inn's dining room. The Rangers followed the Medina on its loop around the town, then rode west along its banks.

The hills grew more rugged as they followed the river's course. Several smaller streams came trickling out of brushy canyons and rocky arroyos to empty into the Medina, and Hank remembered their names from the talk with Sam Knight—Winans Creek, Wallace Creek, Robertson Creek, and Turtle Creek. They spotted several of the animals for which that last one had been named, sunning themselves on deadfalls along the banks. Hank and Casebolt rode a ways up most of the canyons, looking for any sign that a large group of men had passed that way recently. There was none.

They also stopped at most of the cabins they passed, as they had on their way into Bandera the day before. The settlers were more than happy to answer a few questions from a pair of Rangers, but none of them were able to supply any helpful information. As the day wore on, Hank and Casebolt began to come to a conclusion they didn't like.

Isom Whitaker and his men had ridden into the hill country and disappeared.

"They're in here somewhere," Casebolt declared as they paused to rest their horses late in the afternoon. "I can feel it. That son-of-a-bitch is around here laughin' at us."

Hank shook his head. "I don't think so. The gang could have ridden right on through. They could be in San Angelo or Sweetwater by now."

"Maybe," Casebolt grunted. "We still got places to look around here, though." He heeled his horse into motion.

They returned to Bandera a little after sundown, tired and hot and no closer to their goal. As they put their horses away, Hank said, "I hope the Colonel sets as good a table as Mrs. Knight. I'm pretty hungry."

"I could use a drink myself," Casebolt said. "Want to go over to Gersdorff's with me after supper?"

Riding back up Eleventh Street the night before, they had passed the substantial stone building emblazoned GERSDORFF & CO. SALOON, and Casebolt had expressed an interest in the place. Hank grinned and said, "Why not? I want to eat first, though."

"Sure."

As they went into the inn's dining room, Hank asked, "How's the tooth? I noticed you weren't complaining much about it today."

Casebolt grinned and rasped a hand over the silvery stubble on his jaw. "Reckon that lemon extract of Miz Knight's must've worked. There ain't hardly no pain in it at all now."

After the meal, they strolled over toward the saloon, exchanging nods and friendly greetings with the citizens they passed. Hank was aware of the curious stares they were receiving. Knowing how things worked in small towns, he was sure it wouldn't be long until everyone in Bandera knew that there were two Rangers around. If Whitaker *was* in the area, he would hear about their presence. Hank wondered if he and Casebolt should have removed their badges before reaching Bandera. He was so proud to be wearing that silver star on a silver circle that the thought had never occurred to him before. And it was too late to do anything about it now, of course.

The doors were open at Gersdorff's, and plenty of light came past the batwings hung across the entrance. Along with the light came music and laughter, and Casebolt's step quickened as they approached.

The older Ranger swung the batwings open and stepped inside. Hank was right behind him, and as they paused just beyond the door, he saw that the place was typical of most small-town saloons—a rough plank floor covered with sawdust, a long hardwood bar no doubt brought in at great expense, plenty of tables and straight-backed chairs, dozens of bottles with brightly colored labels sitting on the backbar. There were four women circulating among the patrons, bringing them drinks and laughing at their jokes.

Hank and Casebolt went to the bar, each resting one booted foot on the brass rail at its base. A skinny, bald-headed bartender with sweeping moustaches came to take their order. Casebolt said, "Whiskey, and leave the bottle," while Hank settled for a mug of beer drawn from one of the kegs under the bar.

There were probably two dozen customers in the saloon, several of them at the bar and the others scattered around the tables. Most of the men were cowboys from the spreads in the area, but there were also some townsmen and farmers in evidence. Four men were playing cards at one of the tables. None of them appeared to be professional, not from the way they were frowning in concentration at the pasteboards they held.

Hank's beer was dark and cool and good. After his frustrating day it felt good to sip from the mug and relax. Most of the men in the saloon had glanced at them curiously when they entered, but now no one was paying any special attention.

That changed a few minutes later when one of the bar girls sidled up next to him and gave him a bright smile. "Hello," she said. "Can I get you anything?"

Hank lifted the mug of beer in his hand. "I already have a drink, thanks."

The girl's hazel eyes sparkled. "Maybe something else was what I had in mind," she suggested.

Hank winced as Casebolt drove an elbow into his side and grinned. The older Ranger had heard every word the girl was saying, and he knew just as well as Hank did what she meant.

"I don't think so," Hank said gently, not wanting to hurt her feelings. Which was exactly what he wound up doing anyway, he saw.

Her bottom lip came out in a pretty pout. "What's the matter?" she demanded. "Aren't I good-looking enough?"

"Why, I reckon you're lovely, ma'am," Hank lied. "That's not it at all."

She was attractive enough, Hank thought, with a buxom figure and long red hair and a face that was just on the pretty side of plain. But for the last twenty-four hours, the new standard of feminine beauty had been Victoria Knight as far as Hank was concerned.

"Then what is it?" the girl asked, intent on getting an answer.

Hank glanced at Casebolt for help and saw that he was wasting his time. Casebolt was doing good to keep from laughing out loud at Hank's predicament. The least he could have done, Hank thought, was offer to take the girl off his hands.

Something else happened then to get Hank off the hook. One of the men playing poker tossed in his cards with a look of disgust on his face and then seemed to notice for the first time what was going on at the bar. His features hardened into anger, and he shoved his chair back roughly, the legs rasping on the plank floor. Hank saw this over the redhead's shoulder and guessed that he was in for even more trouble. The poker player stood up and stalked toward the bar.

The range clothes he wore hadn't been washed for a long while. A battered black hat was shoved to the back of his head, and there was a dark stubble of beard on his face. A cowhand from one of the nearby ranches, Hank decided, who had ridden into town for a drink and a game of chance and a little female companionship.

"Dammit, Janie," the cowboy snapped. "I thought you said you'd wait for me to play a few hands."

"That was over an hour ago, Wes," the girl replied without looking at him. She kept her eyes on Hank.

"I was lucky for a while," Wes protested. "You don't expect a man to get up from the table while the cards are goin' his way, do you?"

"I suppose that depends on what's really important to him," Janie replied with a contemptuous sniff.

Not wanting any trouble with the cowboy, who had obviously been drinking, Hank drained the last of his beer and placed the mug on the bar. He turned to Casebolt and said quietly, "Come on, Joe."

Before he could move away from the bar, the girl suddenly reached out with both hands and clasped her fingers around his arm. "Don't go yet," she said urgently. "Stay."

Wes took a quick, deep breath and stepped forward. He grabbed one of Janie's hands and yanked it away from Hank's arm. "Stop that!" he said.

"You're not no goddamn whore, and I won't have you acting like one!"

Hank grimaced and glanced again at Casebolt. The older Ranger didn't look so amused now, realizing that this could turn into an ugly incident.

"Look, mister," Hank said in an attempt to head off trouble, "I was just talking to your ladyfriend. I don't want to cause problems for anybody."

"I'm not his ladyfriend!" Janie's voice was getting more strident. "He thinks he owns me just because I've gone with him a few times."

A half turn brought Wes face-to-face with Hank, and a sneer twisted the cowboy's face. "You Rangers," he said with a quick look down at Hank's badge. "You think you can just waltz in somewhere and do as you please and take whatever you want, even it it's somebody else's gal!"

Hank wondered why some of Wes's friends didn't step forward and try to stop him from getting into something he couldn't handle. But then the thought occurred to him that maybe Wes didn't have any friends in this room.

"You'd better just let this go, mister," Hank said in a low voice.

"Why? You afraid to stop hidin' behind that Ranger badge and face me like a man?" Wes's voice was anything but quiet as he issued his challenge.

Hank sighed. There was just so much anybody could take, and he had his own limits. Wes hadn't reached them yet, though. Hank said, "Forget it. I'm leaving." He stepped around a surprised Wes and headed for the doorway.

"The hell you are!" Wes growled. His hand came down on Hank's shoulder and jerked him around.

Hank saw the big fist coming at his face and tried to get out of the way, but he wasn't quite quick enough. The blow clipped him on the side of the head, just above his right ear, knocking him against the bar. Dimly he saw a flicker of movement behind Wes as the cowboy circled to face him again. Then the only thing he saw clearly was the obnoxious young man's hand dipping toward the butt of his gun.

The butt of a Colt slammed into the back of Wes's head before he could reach his own weapon. He let out a groan and pitched forward. Janie gave a short scream and caught him, steering him toward the bar. Wes sagged against it, then slipped down to the floor.

Sheriff Sam Knight stood over the fallen cowboy, gun reversed in his hand. Hank realized that the movement he had seen had been Knight coming into the saloon through the batwings. The sheriff had obviously sized things up in a hurry and acted the best way he knew how to keep someone from getting killed.

Knight looked at Casebolt and said, "You can put that gun away now. This boy's not going to cause any more trouble tonight."

Casebolt nodded. "Don't reckon he is, at that." He slipped his pistol back into its holster as he prodded Wes's unconscious form with a booted toe.

Janie knelt beside the cowboy. She glared up at Knight and said, "Did you have to hit him so hard, Sheriff?"

"Better for Wes to wake up with a headache than not wake up at all," Knight told her. "The boy never should have braced a couple of Rangers, and he damn sure shouldn't have reached for his gun."

"Sorry, Sheriff," Hank told Knight. "I didn't mean to start any trouble. We were just having a drink before we turned in."

Knight shrugged. "Like I said, Wes is a hothead. Reckon it wasn't your fault." He nodded toward Hank's head. "Anyway, you got banged up some, too."

Hank lifted a hand and touched the knot that had quickly come up on the side of his head. It was tender and sore.

"I imagine my wife has just the thing for that goose egg," Knight went on. "You two come on with me, and we'll get it fixed up." He looked across the bar at the bald-headed bartender. "Why don't you let Wes sleep it off in your back room, Dutch?"

"Sure thing, Sheriff," the bartender agreed. He came out from behind the hardwood and motioned for a couple of the customers to help him haul the unconscious cowboy away. Janie went with them.

Knight, Hank, and Casebolt stepped out of the saloon and turned down Eleventh Street. When they were out of earshot of Gersdorff's, Casebolt said, "I'm mighty glad you come along when you did, Sam. I was afraid I was goin' to have to shoot that tadpole."

"I appreciate you not doing it. Would've been a mess, not to mention a waste of a life. I never like to see that." Knight paused, then asked, "Did you have any luck finding Whitaker?"

"Not a sign of him," Casebolt answered disgustedly.

"I've thought of a few more places you might look."

"We'll sure do it," Casebolt said fervently. "I reckon we need all the help we can get, even if a Ranger ain't hardly supposed to say things like that."

"Even the Rangers need a hand from time to time," Hank said, thinking about his father and a showdown in El Paso.

As if reading his mind, Knight said, "Your pa was a Ranger back in the old days, wasn't he, Hank?"

Hank glanced over at the lawman, but in the shadows of evening, it was hard to tell much about Knight's face.

"That's right," Hank admitted. "His name is Enos Littleton."

"I've heard of him," Knight said. "A good man. Reckon you must be, too. That's why I don't mind telling you that my daughter seems to be a bit taken with you."

"Miss Victoria?" The exclamation was out of Hank's mouth before he could stop it. "I figured from the way she was acting last night that she thought I was just some dumb hick."

Knight shook his head. "I know what I saw in her eyes, son. She's a smart girl, and she likes to prod a man a little, find out what he's really like. She hasn't found anybody so far who can really stand up to her."

Hank felt beads of sweat on his forehead, and he knew the night wasn't *that* warm. This conversation was making him uneasy, and he suddenly decided that it might be a better idea to head back to the hotel.

When he tried to say so, though, Knight wouldn't hear of it. "Now, don't let my talk spook you, son," he said. "I just wanted you to know that that gal means the world to me. I don't ever want anybody to hurt her."

"I'd never do that, Sheriff," Hank said.

"He wouldn't, Sam," Casebolt added with a chuckle. "I ain't knowed this boy but a few weeks, but I can tell you already, he's plumb harmless, 'cept when he's got a rifle in his hands. Then you won't never see a better shot. But when it comes to gals . . ."

Hank glared at Casebolt. "Are you defending me or what, Joe?" he demanded.

Casebolt slapped him on the back and laughed. "Come on, son," Casebolt said. "We'd best let the womenfolk take a look at that head of yours 'fore you wind up addlepated."

If he did, he wouldn't be the only addlepated one around here, Hank thought darkly.

Chapter Eight

To Hank's embarrassment, both Faye Knight and her daughter fussed over the bump on his head. Faye dipped a cloth in the water bucket and brought it to Hank, saying, "Here, hold this tight to the knot, so that it won't swell any more." Victoria busied herself asking him questions like what his name was and what the date was, and when he had answered several of them correctly, she declared that there didn't seem to be any mental damage.

"Thanks," Hank said dryly. "I'm glad to know that."

Victoria smiled sweetly. "You can't be too careful."

And Sam Knight had the crazy idea that his daughter liked him, Hank thought. Maybe being sarcastic was Victoria's way of showing that she cared. Maybe she was just trying to cover up the concern she felt for him. He ought to give her the benefit of the doubt.

Casebolt and Knight stood near the table grinning broadly as the two women took care of Hank's injury. They were enjoying his discomfiture, Hank knew, especially Casebolt.

He sat there and held the compress to his head for several minutes, then Faye removed it and said, "There, that's starting to look better. You're still going to have a bump and a bit of a bruise, Mr. Littleton, but I don't think it'll be too bad."

"Thank you, ma'am," Hank nodded. He was conscious of a vague ache behind his eyes, but it was nothing he couldn't put up with for a while.

"Now, you get plenty of rest tonight."

"Yes, ma'am," Hank said meekly, sensing without having to turn around that the grin was growing on Casebolt's weathered face.

"And if you have any other symptoms, like blurred vision or double vision, you'll need to see a doctor," Victoria added.

"Yes, ma'am."

Sam Knight stepped forward and put a hand on Hank's shoulder. "See, I told you these womenfolk would be able to fix you right up, Hank. They've been taking care of me for a long time, and men in our line of work tend to get bunged up more than most folks."

"That's the truth," Casebolt said. "Why, I reckon I've lost track of how many times I've been shot at and stuck with knives and got my head busted."

"It sounds like you've led an extraordinarily violent life, Mr. Casebolt," Faye said.

"Reckon you could say so," Casebolt replied with another grin.

"Just try not to raise too much of a ruckus while you're here in Bandera County, Joe," Knight requested. "Dead bodies make for a lot of paperwork for the local authorities—in this case, me."

Casebolt laughed, then went on in a more serious tone, "You said you had thought of some more places we might look for Whitaker . . . ?"

"That's right," the sheriff said. "Why don't you sit down, and we'll go over them."

Faye took Victoria's arm. "Come along, dear," she said. "We'll get out of the way so the men can talk business."

"But what if I want to listen, Mama?" Victoria asked.

Sam Knight answered the question before his wife had a chance to reply. "This here is the law's business, Victoria, and besides that it's men's business."

"Doesn't seem fair to me," Victoria muttered as she left the room behind her mother and shut the door to the kitchen. A moment later, something slammed inside the kitchen. The three men exchanged knowing glances. To no one's surprise, the kitchen door opened a few seconds later, and Victoria stalked out, hurrying across the room and disappearing through the front door of the house.

"Don't worry about it," Knight told her. "She's just got her back up. She'll get over that."

Knight sat down in his rocking chair, and Casebolt took one of the armchairs. Hank stood up and was about to take the other chair when Casebolt said, "Reckon we don't need you for this little parley, Hank. Sam can tell me about them other places where we need to look. Whyn't you step outside, get some fresh air and rest your head?"

Hank's eyes narrowed in suspicion. He looked from Casebolt to Knight and back again and saw the looks on the faces of the older men. A couple of damn matchmakers, that was what they were. But he was just curious enough about Victoria Knight to take them up on it.

"All right," he said, scooping up his hat from the table. "I'll just do that."

"That's bein' smart," Casebolt said. "Ain't wise to put a strain on your head so soon after gettin' whumped."

Hank didn't put his hat on; he carried it as he went to the front door and let himself out. He pulled the panel shut and then paused on the porch, letting his eyes adjust to the night.

"Did they run off, too?" Victoria's voice asked from the other end of the porch.

Hank turned toward the voice and spotted her shadowy form as she leaned on the railing around the porch. He shrugged his shoulders and said, "Joe and your pa thought they could hash it out without my help. They said they wanted me to rest my brain for a while after getting hit like that."

"It looks like Wes caught you a good one, all right," Victoria said. "He's plenty strong. You're lucky you didn't catch that punch head-on."

"I guess so," Hank said. He sidled closer to her, turning the hat over in his hands.

Victoria shook her head in the gloom. "And all over a tramp like that Janie. Were you really that attracted to her, Mr. Littleton?"

Hank had to control the surge of anger he felt. "It wasn't like that at all," he said. "You're misunderstanding, just like that cowboy did. But I reckon you're doing it on purpose, aren't you?"

"Mr. Littleton!" Victoria said as she caught her breath and swung to face him more directly. "What are you saying?"

"I'm saying that there wasn't a damn thing for anybody to fight over," Hank told her bluntly. "I just talked to that saloon gal for a minute. I wasn't going to buy her a drink or dance with her or . . . or anything else."

"I suppose Janie is pretty enough, in a coarse sort of way. You might have enjoyed yourself."

Without thinking about what he was doing, Hank tossed his hat into the swing that hung from the porch roof. He put both hands on Victoria's shoulders and pulled her closer to him. "Not as much as I'm going to enjoy this."

He brought his mouth down on hers, letting their lips meet in a kiss that suddenly made him a lot dizzier than getting hit on the head.

Victoria stiffened at first, then relaxed in his arms. He felt the warmth of her mouth and her body against his, and a feeling of panic hit him. What the hell was he doing? He had no right to kiss this girl. All she'd done was make fun of him and make him feel like a complete idiot most of the time.

But now she was in his arms, her lips hot and wet under his, the rest of her sort of slowly squirming around. . . .

He took his mouth away from hers and looked down at her, seeing the way the moonlight turned to silver on the soft curve of her cheek. He said, "I'm sorry, Miss Knight. I didn't mean to kiss you. I reckon I'm as addlepated as Joe says I am."

"No," Victoria whispered. "You're not."

And then damned if *she* wasn't kissing *him*.

A few minutes later, as they stood side by side at the porch rail, a little uncomfortable with the intimacy that had taken them both by surprise, Victoria said, "You really did think that Janie was pretty, didn't you?"

"I suppose she is," Hank answered truthfully.

"I shouldn't say bad things about her. She used to be my friend, right after we came here. I didn't know anyone, and she and I are about the same age. I ran into her at Huffmeyers' one day, and we got to talking. I shouldn't hold it against her just because she works in a saloon."

Hank could hear the sincerity and humility in her voice, and that came as even more of a surprise than her actual words. He had a feeling there was a whole lot more to Miss Victoria Knight than he had seen so far in their two meetings. He wouldn't mind getting to know even more about her, he thought.

As a Ranger, he felt guilty for even thinking such things, but the rest of him was intrigued.

The front door squeaked as someone opened it, and Hank and Victoria jumped apart a bit. Casebolt and Knight stepped out onto the porch, and the sheriff said, "You'd best go back inside, Victoria. I hope you haven't been out here pestering Mr. Littleton. He's supposed to be getting some fresh air and resting."

"Miss Victoria's been very pleasant company, sir," Hank said.

Victoria stepped past him, going toward the door. "Good night, Mr. Littleton," she said over her shoulder.

"Good night, ma'am," Hank replied, still savoring the taste of her mouth in his memory.

Her father shut the door behind her, then turned to Hank and asked, "How's the head?"

"Oh, it's hurting a little," Hank replied. "Not too bad, though. Tell Mrs. Knight that I appreciate what she did."

Casebolt settled his hat on his head, then said, "'Preciate all the help you've been givin' us, Sam. We'll check out them other places tomorrow, but I'm startin' to get the feelin' that Whitaker and his bunch just kept on ridin' when they passed through this part of the country. Reckon we can afford a few more days to look around, though."

Hank wanted to heave a sigh of relief when he heard Casebolt's last comment. He had been afraid from the way the older Ranger was talking that they might be moving on themselves in another day or so. He picked up his hat from the swing and put it on carefully.

"Well, if you don't mind my saying so," Knight went on, "I hope they aren't around here. Bandera's been a peaceful place of late, and I'd like for it to stay that way."

Casebolt paused on the steps, one foot higher than the other. He looked back up at Knight and said, "You know, Sam, ever since I met you I've been thinkin' that I ought to know you for some reason or other. Your name's mighty familiar. Somethin' about some outlaw . . ." Casebolt's voice trailed off as he mused, and then suddenly he snapped his fingers. "Hell, I recollect what it was now! It just come to me! Happened up in Bandera Pass, didn't it?"

For a long moment, Sam Knight said nothing. Then he gave a heavy sigh and replied, "That's right."

Hank frowned. He remembered Casebolt telling him about the battle at Bandera Pass between Captain Jack Hays's Texas Rangers and a band of Comanche Indians, but that had happened over thirty years ago, long before Sam Knight was sheriff of Bandera County.

Knowing it was somewhat impolite to indulge his curiosity, Hank asked, "Excuse me, Sheriff, but what's Joe talking about?"

Casebolt answered the question himself. "Sam here tracked down some owlhoot who was raisin' hell all over the hill country. Finally caught him up in Bandera Pass and traded lead with him."

"And he got away," Knight concluded, bitterness edging into his voice. "That was a year ago, but when the weather's right my arm still hurts from the bullet I took."

Casebolt nodded. "I heard about it, all right. I was workin' up in Fort Worth as a jailer, and I recollect some of the boys talkin' about it. There was somethin' else, though . . ."

"Just the usual shoot-out between a sheriff and an outlaw," Knight insisted. "Like I said, the fella got away, but he hasn't been seen around here since."

"No, I'm sure there was something else," Casebolt said, rubbing his jaw in deep thought.

For some reason, Hank felt compelled to reach out and grasp his partner's arm. "Come on, Joe," he said quickly. "I'm pretty tuckered out. I want to get some sleep."

Sam Knight's face was taut in the moonlight, and Hank knew then why he wanted to leave. Casebolt was poking at something that Knight didn't want disturbed, and Hank liked the sheriff enough to want to honor that.

But Casebolt looked up and said softly, "Goddamn, it was your brother."

Knight's head jerked in a nod. "That's right. My twin brother Russ was that owlhoot. I knew it, knew it when I set out after him. He turned bad early, left home and started robbing—and killing." The sheriff took a deep breath. Hank wished he would stop, but he went on, "I always thought maybe that was why I took up being a lawman, to try to make up for what Russ was doing. I used to hear about jobs he had pulled, and I always prayed that we'd never run across each other. No matter what else he was, he was still my brother, and I damn sure didn't want to face him over the barrel of a gun. That's the way it worked out, though. He stopped the stagecoach between here and Junction, robbed the express box, shot the driver. There was nothing else I could do but go after Russ. But—like I said—he got away." A humorless smile twisted Knight's features. "I reckon it threw my aim off a little, looking in a mirror like that. Didn't seem to bother Russ's."

Hank could have kicked Casebolt right at that moment. Sam Knight had done nothing but try to help them, and in return Casebolt had stirred up some obviously painful memories. The older Ranger didn't look too pleased with himself, either. He grimaced and stared down at the porch.

"Sorry, Sam," he muttered.

Knight laughed hollowly. He slapped Casebolt on the shoulder. "Hell, don't worry about it, Joe. It's all over and done with now, and like I said, Russ lit out and hasn't shown his face around here since. I don't reckon he ever will."

There was nothing else for Hank or Casebolt to say. Casebolt had said more than enough already, Hank thought. He said quietly, "Come on, Joe."

The two Rangers had reached the bottom of the steps when the sound of hoofbeats came to their ears. Sam Knight heard them, too, and paused on the porch. All three men looked down Eleventh Street toward the sound.

"Somebody's in a hurry," Casebolt said.

Hank thought the same thing, and the lawman's instincts that had begun to develop in him told him that a lone rider galloping through the night might mean trouble. As the hoofbeats grew louder, the rider emerged from the darkness and raced up to the house, pulling his horse to a sliding stop that raised a silvery cloud of dust in the moonlight.

"Sheriff!" the man called out as he flung himself from the saddle. "That you, Sheriff?"

Knight came down off the porch and caught the man's arm. "Hold on there, mister!" he snapped. "Who are you, and what's wrong?"

"You . . . you know me, Sheriff," the man said, gasping for breath after what had clearly been a long, hard ride. "I'm Arnie Schwartz, from down at Hondo Canyon."

"Sure, I remember you now, Arnie," Knight said. He glanced over at Hank and Casebolt. "Hondo Canyon's a settlement southwest of here," he told them. "Now, Arnie, what's the matter?"

The man reached up and sleeved sweat from his face. The night hadn't cooled off much so far. Arnie was wearing shoes and corduroy pants and a homespun shirt, and he looked like the farmer that he undoubtedly was. His horse had the look of a draft animal, too, but he had been getting some good speed out of it.

"They came into town this evening and robbed the hotel!" The words tumbled out of Arnie's mouth. "They shot the place up something fierce, Sheriff. I think people might've got killed. I ain't sure. Folks sent me to fetch you right away, right after those owlhoots rode out."

Hank felt his heart pounding in his chest, and when he glanced over at Casebolt, he could see the excitement on the older Ranger's face.

"Do you know who it was, Arnie?" Knight demanded. "Do you know who the robbers were?"

The man shook his head. "I ain't got no earthly idea, Sheriff. All I know was what I saw. There was nearly a dozen of 'em, and they come in almost like they was soldiers or somethin'. They all had on long coats, too, and I thought that was sort of funny, since it was hot and all. Then they started shootin'. . . . Hell, it was awful."

"I reckon it was, Arnie," Knight said softly. "I reckon it was."

And Hank and Casebolt looked at each other and said at the same moment, "Whitaker."

Chapter Nine

"Come on in the house, Arnie," Sheriff Knight told the man who had brought word of the robbery from Hondo Canyon. "You look worn out from that ride. A cup of my wife's coffee will fix you up." As Knight steered Arnie Schwartz toward the porch, he glanced over his shoulder at Hank and Casebolt. "I reckon you two want to go with me."

Casebolt nodded. "We'll get our hosses."

"I'll meet you in front of the hotel in five minutes," Knight said.

"We'll be ready."

Hank and Casebolt started toward the Riverside Inn, their fast walk threatening to turn into a run. Hank had forgotten all about his headache.

It took only moments for Casebolt and him to get their horses saddled up and ready to ride. The few people on the street this evening cast curious glances toward the two Rangers.

Hank and Casebolt had to wait only a minute or so before Sam Knight came cantering up on a sturdy-looking bay mare, a Winchester lying across the saddle in front of him. His face was grim as he asked, "Ready?"

"Lead the way," Casebolt told him.

The route between Bandera and Hondo Canyon was a little more than a trail and a little less than a road. Hank, Casebolt, and Knight made good time on it, Knight taking the lead. There was plenty of light from the moon and stars for the men to see where they were going. When they had covered a little over ten miles, Hank judged, he spotted lights up ahead and knew they were approaching the settlement.

Hondo Canyon was still in an uproar when they rode into the little town a few minutes later. The settlement consisted of one short street with houses and a few businesses along each side, the most prominent of which was the hotel. It was a two-story frame building with a steep roof and a covered porch. That porch was choked with men at the moment, most of them gesturing wildly and seemingly intent on shouting down everyone else. All along the street, lanterns were lit in the buildings and houses. Even though several hours had passed since the raid, excitement was running strong in Hondo Canyon.

Sam Knight rode up to the men on the hotel porch and lifted his voice. "Hold it!" he bellowed. "Hold it down there! Somebody tell me what's going on."

The racket on the porch died down to a chorus of muttering. A slender, middle-aged man in a brown suit and a limp white shirt stepped forward. He looked up at Knight and said fervently, "Thank God you're here, Sheriff. Maybe now we can get after those thieves."

Knight leaned on the pommel of his saddle. "Getting up a posse, are you, Hampton?" he asked.

"Well . . . of course. We have to go after them. They stole a thousand dollars of my money, and who knows how much from my guests."

Casebolt spoke up, "You're the owner of this here hotel?"

"That's right," the man snapped. "Who're y—" He broke off as he saw the badges shining in the light that spilled out of the hotel. "Oh. Rangers, eh? Well, you're certainly in the right place at the right time. You can lend a hand in tracking down those desperadoes."

"I'm not chasing nobody in the dark until I know more about them," Knight said. "Now, tell me about the robbery."

That question touched off a new wave of shouting as the townsmen each tried to spin his own version of the story. Knight lifted a hand and waved them down, then said, "All right, let Hampton tell it."

72

The hotel owner pulled a handkerchief from his pocket and wiped sweat off his face. "They rode in just as most of the guests were finishing dinner. Many of them were still in the dining room, in fact. I was at the desk in the lobby, and when I saw them ride up outside I thought perhaps they were looking for lodging for the night."

"How many were there?" Casebolt asked.

"Nine or ten. I'm not sure of the exact number, because some of them immediately pulled their guns and stayed outside to keep anyone from interfering. The others stormed in and demanded that I give them all the money in the hotel safe. Three or four of them entered the dining room and started relieving all the guests of their valuables. It was a horrible experience, Sheriff, just horrible. I'll never forget the look on the leader's face as he glared at me over the barrel of his gun."

Hank felt an instinctive dislike for the fussy little man, but the hotel owner had seen the leader of the gang at close range and therefore possessed a valuable piece of information.

"What did the man look like?" Hank asked.

Hampton glanced over at Hank and sniffed. "He was big and ugly," he said. "I could tell that much, even though a bandanna was tied across the lower half of his face. His hat was pushed back slightly, and I could see that he had red hair, curly red hair."

Hank's insides tightened. That description fitted Whitaker, all right. It could also fit a dozen other outlaws, but given the fact that Whitaker and his men had fled in this direction from the train robbery south of San Antonio, Hank was convinced that it had indeed been the renegade former State Policeman.

He looked at Casebolt and gave a curt nod, confirming what both of them had suspected all along.

Knight said, "How did the shooting get started?"

"I was going to hand over the money with no trouble, of course," Hampton replied, "but one of the guests tried to resist. I'm told he reached for a gun under his coat, and one of the men shot him down like a dog. I suppose that spooked the men waiting outside, because one of them fired at old Mr. Darby for no good reason. The shot hit him and killed him instantly."

Knight grimaced and shook his head. "Damn. Old Darby wouldn't hurt anybody, even if he wasn't ninety years old."

"Whitaker and his men operate like that, Sheriff," Hank said. "Whitaker's always been quick to shoot."

Knight glanced at Hank. "You sound like you know the man," he said.

"I used to," Hank replied. This wasn't the time or place to go into the history of his relationship with Whitaker, so he went on, "I'm convinced it was the gang we're after, Sheriff. What are our chances of being able to trail them tonight?"

"Not good," Knight said flatly. "We'd best wait until morning and see if we can pick up their tracks then. Otherwise we might be riding into an ambush, even if we could follow their sign—which I doubt."

"You mean you're just going to let them get away?" Hampton demanded, outraged. "But what about my money?"

"I hope you get it back sooner or later," Knight told him. "But I'm still not going to go charging off half-cocked in the middle of the night with a posse full of townsfolk at my back. That's a good way to get killed."

From the glaring and the muttering of the crowd, it was clear that the sheriff's decision was widely unpopular. Still, when he glanced over at Casebolt, Hank saw that the older Ranger was nodding in agreement.

"We'll try to pick up their trail first thing in the morning," Knight went on, addressing all the men now. "Any of you who want to ride with me be here an hour after sunup. And come armed."

The townies nodded, some of them still complaining under their breath. Overall, though, there was a feeling of relief in the crowd. For all their excitement, they knew deep down it would have been dangerous trying to track the bandits at night.

Hampton opened his mouth to complain again, then shut it without saying anything else. He shook his head and turned to go back into the hotel. The knot of men on the porch broke up and dispersed quickly.

Casebolt leaned forward in his saddle and asked Knight, "Are you headin' back to Bandera tonight, Sam?"

"I thought I would," Knight nodded. "It'll mean some extra riding, but I don't want to leave Faye and Victoria alone overnight unless I have to."

"Reckon Hank and I will just stay here. We'll try and get a head start on you in the mornin'. If we can pick up those tracks, we can blaze a trail for you and make it easier for you to follow with that posse.''

"Sounds like a good idea." Knight gave a hollow laugh. "I'm not too fond of the idea of taking all those men along anyway, but I knew they'd insist on going."

Casebolt nodded. "If we find Whitaker first, we'll hold off and let you catch up 'fore we try to take him."

"That's fine." Knight turned his horse and lifted a hand in farewell. "See you tomorrow." He rode off, following the trail northeast out of town.

Casebolt turned to Hank. "I hope that was all right with you, son, tellin' Knight we'd stay here, I mean."

Hank shrugged. "No reason not to do it this way, is there?"

A sly grin tugged at Casebolt's mouth. "Well, if we was to've stayed in Bandera, you might've got an invite to breakfast at the sheriff's house in the mornin'."

Hank thought about Victoria Knight for a moment, wondering what she would look like early in the morning. Then he shook his head and said, "With us this close to Whitaker, Joe, breakfast is the last thing I'm worried about. Now why don't we go inside and see if that Hampton fella will rent us some rooms for the night?"

Hampton was more than happy to rent them a pair of rooms on the ground floor of the hotel. There was no stable, but Hank and Casebolt tied their horses around back and took their gear to their rooms with them.

Several times, the hotel owner demanded assurances that they would catch the robbers. "We'll do what we can, mister," Casebolt told him. "Now how about lettin' us get some sleep? You don't want to be arrested for disturbin' the peace in your own hotel."

Hampton withdrew in a hurry after that, and the two Rangers were left alone. Hank tried to sleep, but it was a long time in coming. The chance that they might catch up to Whitaker the next day kept his mind whirling. He didn't even think too much about Victoria Knight.

He and Casebolt pulled out when the sun was barely over the eastern horizon the next morning. There hadn't been much traffic in or out of Hondo Canyon after the robbery, so it was fairly easy to spot the tracks of a large group of men riding west out of the settlement. As the sun rose and grew hotter, Hank and Casebolt followed the trail, pausing occasionally to leave markers for Knight and the posse.

As they left the Medina Valley, the ground became rockier, the hills more rugged, and the trails more choked with brush. By noon, even Casebolt had to admit that they had lost the trail, but he and Hank pushed on, hoping that the outlaws had continued heading in the same general direction.

Around mid-afternoon, the Rangers reached a small community called Vanderpool, on the Sabinal River. The night before, Sam Knight had mentioned that they might try looking for Whitaker in the Sabinal Valley. Vanderpool was a tiny place, but it was large enough to have a general store, and sitting on the porch was a man holding his head in his hands. There was a blood-stained rag tied around his head, Hank saw as they reined in.

"Howdy, mister," Casebolt said. "Looks like you had some trouble."

The man looked up at them dully. He wore the apron of a storekeeper and had a tuft of whiskers on his chin. "You ain't more of them, are you?" he asked.

"More of who?"

"Those men who came in here and robbed me." The storekeeper pointed to the bloody cloth on his head. "Gave me this, one of them did, when I didn't hop fast enough."

"How long ago was this?" Hank wanted to know.

"An hour maybe. I don't know. My head hurts too bad to worry about it."

Hank and Casebolt exchanged glances. They had been thinking that Whitaker and his men had a lot longer lead on them than one hour. Casebolt mused, "They must've holed up somewheres the biggest part of the day."

Hank nodded. "But now they're on the move again." He turned his attention back to the injured man. "What did those men steal from you? Money?"

"What little bit I had," came the dispirited answer. "Wasn't much. Mostly they took supplies. Flour, sugar, coffee, things like that. Damn near cleaned me out of bacon, they did."

"They've been hiding out most of the time since that railroad job," Hank speculated to Casebolt. "They only came back out because their supplies were running low."

"That's what it sounds like to me, too, right enough," Casebolt agreed. He asked the storekeeper, "Which way did they go when they lit out of here?"

The man waved vaguely toward the northeast. "Yonder, I think. I wasn't paying too much attention at the time, seeing as I was laying on the floor with my head caved in."

Hank glanced up and down Vanderpool's single street. He didn't see a single soul except the storekeeper. "Where is everybody?"

"Still hiding out, I imagine. The way that bunch went whooping and shooting out of here, you'd think a war had started up again."

There was no doubt in Hank's mind that the outlaws who had raided Vanderpool's only store had been Whitaker and his men. He could tell that Casebolt shared that opinion. He said to the storekeeper, "We're Texas Rangers, mister, and we're on the trail of that bunch. Don't worry, we'll catch up to them."

The man stared doubtfully at them and waved a hand toward the hills again. "Out there? If they get up in those canyons along the West Prong of the Medina, you could hunt for a year and not root them out. No, sir, you won't find them." He dropped his head back into his hands.

Hank and Casebolt didn't try to argue with him. They just turned their horses around and rode out of Vanderpool.

Sam Knight and the posse from Hondo Canyon probably weren't too far behind them now. They decided to follow their own back trail until they met up with the posse; there was no point in Knight and the others riding all the way to Vanderpool when it appeared that Whitaker's gang was swinging north in a rough circle.

In less than an hour, Hank and Casebolt met Knight and the posse in a meadow alongside one of the countless creeks in the area. Knight held up his hand to bring his group to a halt when he spotted the two Rangers riding toward them. "Any luck?" he asked as Hank and Casebolt drew rein.

"Not much," Hank said. "Whitaker and his men held up a store in Vanderpool and headed northeast from there."

Knight glanced in that direction and bit off a curse. "That's the ruggedest part of the county," he said. "Reckon we've got to try to track them, though."

Several members of the posse looked distinctly unhappy at that suggestion. One of them said, "Look, Sheriff, it's gettin' late, and I've got to get back home before it gets too dark." A few others murmured similar complaints.

"All right." Knight nodded wearily. "Any of you boys who wants to head back, just go right ahead. There'll be no hard feelings."

"Thanks, Sheriff," one of the men said. He turned his horse and headed back toward Hondo Canyon.

Slowly, the others trailed after him, leaving Hank, Casebolt, and Knight alone.

The sheriff heaved a sigh. "That's the way it is with posses," he said. "If you can catch whoever you're after pretty quick, they do just fine."

"I don't guess you can blame them," Hank said. "They're just worried about their own folks."

"Oh, I don't blame them, Hank," Knight replied. "Shoot, they're only volunteers." He grinned. "You two up to some more hard riding?"

"Reckon we'll have to be," Casebolt replied.

The three of them headed north, swinging around a peak Knight identified as Flat Top Mountain. As promised, the terrain became even rougher as they hit the West Prong of the Medina River and began to follow it eastward. After a while, Hank started to wonder if he would remember what it was like to ride on level ground again. It seemed he had been going uphill or downhill all his life. He had to admit that the scenery was pretty spectacular, what with the twisting canyons and the rugged, tree-covered hills.

But there was no sign of Isom Whitaker and his men. Once again, the outlaws had vanished, and it was three exhausted, disappointed lawmen who rode back into Bandera in the middle of the night.

Chapter Ten

That was just the start of a frustrating few days for Hank Littleton and
Joe Casebolt. The Rangers spent part of that time searching the rugged
hills northwest of Bandera. Now that Isom Whitaker and his men had
emerged from hiding, there were more frequent reports of their being
seen, but Hank and Casebolt always seemed to get there too late. The
gang would appear, pull another robbery, and then fade away into the
cedar-dotted canyons. The stagecoach on the regular run between Bandera and San Antonio was hit twice, both times by men matching the
description of Whitaker's bunch.

Maybe Captain McNelly's faith in them hadn't been justified after all,
Hank brooded as he sat on the front porch of Schmidtke and Hay's store
one afternoon. Casebolt, Knight, and George Hay were sitting there as
well, discussing Whitaker's activities.

Hank kept his mouth shut. His first major job as a Ranger, and he had
failed. The notion was a bitter one for him to swallow.

"No offense, Rangers," the storekeeper was commenting, "but this
country is just too blasted big for two men to track down anybody."

Casebolt spat into the dust of the street. "Don't see what good more men would do," he said.

"You could spread out more, cover more ground when you're searching."

"And then who'd handle the Injuns and the rest of the desperadoes 'tween here and the border?" Casebolt sighed. "I don't know, Hay, maybe you're right."

"We'll catch up to Whitaker's bunch sooner or later," Knight said. "Folks all over the county have been told to keep an eye out for him now. It's just a matter of time until somebody sees something that'll help us nab him."

Hank hoped that was true, but he was starting to have his doubts.

That evening, as he and Casebolt were having dinner in the hotel dining room, Colonel Duffy came in from the lobby and looked around until he spotted them. He came over to their table and extended a slip of paper. "The sheriff sent this message over for you, Mr. Casebolt."

Casebolt unfolded the paper, squinted at it, and then passed it over to Hank. "You need to get some more lanterns in this place, Colonel," he groused. "There ain't hardly enough light in here for me to read that."

Hank grinned, knowing the real reason Casebolt had handed him the message. He looked over the writing on the paper and saw that Sheriff Knight was requesting that they come over to his office right away.

Pushing back his chair, Hank got to his feet. "Thanks, Colonel," he told Duffy. "Come on, Joe, the sheriff wants to see us."

Casebolt looked down at his food. "But I'm not finished eatin'!" he protested.

Hank shrugged and said, "Sounds important."

"Oh, all right," Casebolt grumbled. As he stood up, he snagged an ear of corn off his plate and carried it out with him, gnawing on it as he and Hank walked down the street toward the county office building.

When they reached it, the lantern was lit in Sam Knight's office, and the sheriff was sitting behind his desk listening to a man in his late twenties who was dressed as a cowhand. The man was saying, ". . . told me about this fella Whitaker. That's when I decided I ought to come see you, Sheriff."

"And I'm glad you did, Jim," Knight grunted. He looked up at Hank and Casebolt and grinned. "Howdy, boys. We might finally have the break we needed to help us latch on to Whitaker." He indicated the cowhand. "This is Jim Teague, from up Camp Verde way. Jim, these men are Rangers Casebolt and Littleton. Why don't you tell them what you just told me?"

"Sure," Teague nodded. "Like I was sayin' to Sheriff Knight, I saw a bunch of strangers ridin' up close to Camp Verde today. Wasn't sure what they were up to, so I got off my hoss and stayed in some brush until they was past. Watched 'em ride up to one of the hills overlookin' the store. They looked the place over real good, then left. I went on down to the store, and there was some folks there talkin' about this Whitaker. From what Sheriff Knight tells me about him, I'd say he was the one leadin' that bunch."

"They just looked over the store and then left?" Casebolt asked, a frown on his face. He licked the last of the butter from the corn off his fingers.

"That's right."

"Getting the lay of the land, that would be my guess," Knight put in. "I reckon they plan to hit it tomorrow."

"Why tomorrow?" Hank wanted to know. "Why not just rob it today, since they were already there?"

"Because the stage from Kerrsville will be stopping there at noon tomorrow. And I happen to know that the Rothe brothers are having some money shipped in from Brady to make the payroll for their hands. They've got the biggest spread around here, so it's liable to be a considerable amount."

Hank and Casebolt looked at each other. The prospect of hitting a ranch payroll would be too tempting for Whitaker to pass up.

"What's up there at Camp Verde now?" Casebolt asked. "The old post is closed down, ain't it?"

"That's right," Knight nodded. "Nothing there now but the store where the road fords Verde Creek."

Jim Teague added, "The camp never amounted to much after the army took the camels away. The ones that was still there, I mean, not the ones that had already gone wild."

Casebolt snorted. "Wild camels? I been hearin' that story for years, but I don't reckon there's a lick of truth in it."

Teague's face reddened. "Ranger or not, you can't call me a liar, mister. I helped herd them beasts, and I'm here to tell you there was more than a few that run off into the hills. Reckon some of 'em are still out there.''

Casebolt held up his hands and said, "No offense, son. I reckon you saw what you saw. It's just that I ain't goin' to believe in them wild camels until I see one with my own eyes.''

The cowhand still looked a bit put out by Casebolt's doubts, but he made no reply. Knight said, "Seems to me like what you two need to do is make sure you're at the Camp Verde store tomorrow. I don't imagine Whitaker is expecting any trouble, so you could sure as hell surprise him.''

"What about you, Sam?'' Casebolt asked.

Knight shook his head. "The camp's out of my jurisdiction. It's right over the line in Kerr County. You might be able to get some help from the sheriff up in Kerrsville, though.''

Casebolt shook his head. "Reckon Hank and I can handle this by ourselves. We'll ride up there first thing in the mornin' and get set up. With any luck, we can take Whitaker and his bunch without firin' a shot.''

Knight stood up. "Well, good luck. Happen you do catch them, why don't you bring them back down here? We've got a good solid jail, and Bandera's closer than Kerrsville. Besides, it's my county that Whitaker's been raising hell in until now.''

From the look on Knight's face, Hank could tell the sheriff wanted to be in on Whitaker's capture. Sam Knight followed the law, though, and the law said he had no authority at Camp Verde. Ranger badges, on the other hand, were good anywhere in the state.

"We'll tote 'em back down here, all right,'' Casebolt agreed. "Thanks for lettin' us know about this, Sam. And thanks to you, too, Mr. Teague.''

Teague grinned, his anger of a few moments earlier forgotten now. "Glad to help,'' he said.

Hank and Casebolt said their good nights and headed back to the hotel. Hank could feel his pulse racing. After more than a week, they might be on the verge of bringing this assignment to a successful conclusion. Maybe he should have been more patient, he thought, but he was more than ready to see Isom Whitaker behind bars. The man had a lot to answer for.

Maybe justice was finally going to catch up to him.

Not surprisingly, Hank did not sleep well. He was too excited about the prospect of capturing Whitaker and his gang. It was far into the night before he finally dozed off.

Despite the lack of sleep, Hank was alert the next morning. He and Casebolt ate a quick breakfast and were on the trail out of Bandera before the sun had been up an hour. They rode up the bluff to the north of town, and a little farther on crossed Bandera Creek. The terrain here was fairly flat, with hills in the distance all around. Far to the northeast were the Twin Sisters, and directly ahead of them was the range that divided the valleys of the Medina and Guadalupe Rivers. Bandera Pass was clearly visible in the morning sunshine, its edges as sharp as if someone had taken a giant knife and carved a wedge out of the hills.

"We'll get the lay of the land ourselves," Casebolt said as they rode. "Probably put one of us inside the store and the other outside somewhere. Shouldn't be too hard to get the drop on Whitaker and his men."

"Maybe we should have tried to get some help from Kerr County, like Sheriff Knight suggested," Hank commented.

Casebolt shook his head. "Whitaker's our job."

Hank nodded and fell silent.

Despite the fact that the pass was fairly deep, the trail leading up to it followed a steep angle for several hundred yards. As they rode through the gap, Hank glanced from side to side at the rocky, brush-covered slopes. There were plenty of places for ambushers to hide, and he was reminded of Casebolt's story about the battle here between the Rangers and the Comanches. Hank could picture it vividly, the heat and blood, the dust filling the air, the crash of guns and savage whoops of the Indians.

This was also where Sam Knight had caught up with his twin brother and been forced to trade shots with him. It was hard to believe that a man as upstanding as Sheriff Knight could have such a close relative who was an outlaw. But there was never any way of knowing how somebody was going to turn out, no way to predict what path a person would take in life. If things had gone differently for him, he supposed that he could have wound up on the wrong side of the law, too, despite the fact that his father had been a Ranger and his grandfather the sheriff of San Saba County.

Verde Creek was about three miles beyond the pass. Like the other streams in the area, it was lined with massive cypresses drooping over the water. Hank and Casebolt splashed their mounts across the ford and up the bank to the Camp Verde store. It was a square, solid-looking stone building with two stories. Sturdy wooden pillars supported a balcony over the front porch. The balcony was roofed in as well, and on that roof was a short flagpole with the Stars and Stripes fluttering from it in the breeze. A long wooden sign attached to the balcony railing proclaimed that this was the Camp Verde General Store. A wagon was parked in front of the place, and several horses were tied at the hitch rack.

Hank and Casebolt swung down from their saddles and tied their mounts there as well, then stepped into the place. It was dim inside, and cool, due to the thickness of the stone walls. Like most general stores, it contained a little bit of everything that would be needed to make life bearable on an isolated ranch or farm.

The proprietor was a bushy-whiskered man, who was waiting on a man and woman, the couple no doubt having come in the wagon from one of the nearby spreads. The cowboys whose horses were tied up outside were browsing around the store, stealing as much time away from their chores as they could.

The man behind the counter glanced up as Hank and Casebolt entered, then looked again as he spotted their badges. He finished selling a bag of coffee to the couple, then turned to Hank and Casebolt and asked, "What can I do for you fellas?"

"We're here on law business," Casebolt said curtly. "Reckon we could talk in your back room for a minute?"

"Sure," the man nodded. He called out to the cowboys, "You jaspers keep your cotton-pickin' hands off things while I'm gone, you hear?"

He led the way past the counter and through a door into a storeroom. Keeping his voice low, Casebolt said, "My partner and I have a hunch you're goin' to have some trouble here today when the stage from Kerrsville comes in. We're goin' to be on hand to put a stop to it, though. You heard of a fella called Whitaker?"

The proprietor paled slightly under his heavy growth of beard. "That outlaw who's been raising so much hell down Bandera way? Damn right I've heard of him. He's not around here now, is he?"

"That's what we've heard," Casebolt said.

The man grimaced and uttered a heartfelt curse, then reached out for a shotgun that was leaning in one corner. "Let the bastard come," he said. "He'll get a warm welcome, let me tell you."

Casebolt held up his hands. "Now just hold on a minute, mister. That gang'd just shoot you down and not give it another thought." He grinned. "The boy and I got ourselves a plan, though. . . ."

Chapter Eleven

By the time the sun was directly overhead, Hank's rear end was hurting considerably. Sitting on a hard tree limb would do that to a man. Hank shifted a little, slowly and carefully so that the motion wouldn't set the cypress leaves to swaying too much. There was a little breeze already, and that helped conceal his movements.

He had been sitting up in this tree on the bank of Verde Creek for several hours now while Casebolt waited inside the store in comfort. The older Ranger had pointed out that they needed to get into position early, in case Whitaker had somebody scout out the scene before the noon stage arrived. That had made sense to Hank, and so had the idea that he would be the one to wait in the tree. After all, he was considerably younger and spryer.

But he was still tired, and he was glad when he peered to the north and saw the plume of dust spiraling up from the trail. The stage was coming.

And if they were right, Whitaker and his gang would not be far behind.

Hank's post in the tree commanded a view of the store, some fifty feet away. The thick foliage would conceal him until Whitaker and his men made their move. Then, if all went according to plan, Casebolt would throw down on them from inside the store while Hank would catch them in a crossfire from behind.

The stage from Kerrsville came barreling down the trail, a traditional Concord coach with a six-horse team. It rocked and swayed on its leather thoroughbraces, the hooves of the team and the iron-bound wheels kicking up a cloud of dust. Hank saw the driver and a shotgun guard sitting on the box and hoped there weren't many passengers inside. It might get dangerous around here if bullets started flying. Luckily, there were no customers inside the store just now.

The driver applied the brake and slowed his team as the coach neared the creek. He swung the horses toward the store and brought the coach to a halt in front of the old stone building. Leaning over, he called out, "Camp Verde, folks. We'll just be stopped for a few minutes to rest the team, so don't wander off."

It was a shame they hadn't been able to let the driver and the guard know what was happening, Hank thought. That might have helped. They would just have to rely on the professionalism of the two men. If they had been working on stagecoach runs for very long, they had no doubt encountered hold-up attempts before.

What if Whitaker didn't even show up? That question suddenly occurred to Hank. Surely all their preparations hadn't been for nothing.

His grip tightened on the Henry rifle in his hands as he heard the sound of hoofbeats. The sound came from the west, upstream.

The riders emerged from a stand of trees along a bend of the creek. There were nine of them, Hank saw as he leaned forward tensely. They wore long coats that flapped in the breeze, and the man in the lead was big and redheaded, with a sunburned face.

Whitaker.

Hank remembered him, all right. He hadn't changed much since Hank had seen him last. Hank scanned the faces of the other men as best he could through the screen of branches and leaves.

As his gaze reached the man on the other end of the line from Whitaker, Hank got a shock that made him grip the rifle in his hands until his fingers whitened.

The last man was Brian Parrish.

Hank remembered Brian from San Saba, too. He was still tall, slender, bearded, and handsome. Back in the days when they had both been kids playing along the San Saba River, Brian hadn't had the beard, of course, but otherwise he looked much the same. Hank had never been able to understand why Brian had wanted to do a damn-fool thing like go off and join the State Police.

But that was exactly what Brian Parrish had done, and the next time Hank saw him, he was riding with Isom Whitaker on a mission that was nothing less than murder. Legal at the time, maybe, but still murder.

Brian hadn't taken part in the shooting, Hank remembered. But he had been there when Whitaker and the other members of the State Police troop had gunned down the men they were after without even giving them a chance to surrender. In his memory, Hank could see the bloody scene as plain as day, and he recalled the cold stares he and Brian Parrish had exchanged, their friendship lost.

And now Parrish was still riding with Whitaker. He was willing to bet that Brian had learned to kill by now, too.

Hank glanced back at the stagecoach. The driver had climbed down off the box, and the passengers were disembarking and going up the steps into the store. There were two men, who seemed to be traveling alone, and a family of a man, a woman, and three children. The children paused and looked curiously at the men riding up, and Hank held his breath for a moment until their mother shooed them on into the store. Behind those thick walls they would be safe enough, if they stayed away from the windows and door.

The shotgun guard was still standing on the box, and he had turned to face the approaching riders. Hank could see the taut way the man held both himself and the greener. The guard was prepared for trouble, but Hank doubted he was ready for the kind that Whitaker could give him.

Whitaker held up his hand and then reined in, bringing his horse to a stop about ten feet behind the coach. The other members of the gang followed suit. The guard watched them over the roof of the vehicle. Hank was close enough to hear the words quite plainly as Whitaker said, "Afternoon, friend. Just get in from Kerrsville?"

"That's right," the guard replied curtly.

Whitaker folded his hands on the saddlehorn and grinned. "In that case, why don't you just climb down off that thing and step out of the way? The boys and I intend to take what you're carrying."

A muscle twitched in Hank's grim face as he looked on from the tree.

Whitaker was bold as brass, that was for sure. And he had that sly smile on his face that Hank remembered all too well.

The guard stared at Whitaker for a long moment, then said, "You're crazy, mister. Nobody's taking anything from this stage."

So far none of the outlaws had drawn their guns. Hank could see that all of them had their hands hovering near the butts of their pistols, though. Whitaker just kept grinning and said, "That's where you're wrong."

A new voice cracked from the store. "No, Whitaker, *you're* wrong!" Joe Casebolt called out, and the words were followed by the unmistakable sound of a cartridge being levered into a rifle chamber. "Don't any of you move."

Several of the gang stiffened and started to reach for their guns, but Whitaker stopped them with a slash of his hand and a sharp "Hold it!" He turned his head to look at the store and saw the rifle barrel protruding from one of the windows. From a window on the other side of the door came the twin muzzles of a shotgun and the long barrel of a Remington revolver. The storekeeper and the stagecoach driver were taking a hand in this game, too.

Up on the box, the guard cast a nervous glance around. As things stood, he seemed to be hung out to dry. The men in the store could inflict heavy casualties on the gang, but he would almost certainly be hit in the shooting.

Hank made his move, thrusting the barrel of the Henry forward and working the lever. The noise was enough to make the outlaws look in his direction and see that they would be caught in a crossfire if they started shooting. The distraction gave the guard time to drop to his knees. He crouched there on the floorboard of the box, out of the line of fire for the moment but in a position to rise up and let loose with both barrels of the scattergun across the top of the coach.

Whitaker considered the situation for a moment, then abruptly laughed. "Pretty smooth, mister, whoever you are," he called into the store. "But you know good and well you can't drop all of us."

"We can sure as hell get you, though, Whitaker," Casebolt replied. "And for your information, the name's Joe Casebolt. I'm a Texas Ranger."

Hank saw Whitaker's face tighten. The outlaw knew he couldn't expect any kind of break from a Ranger.

The other members of the gang were just as tense as their leader. It was all some of them could do not to grab for their guns and start blasting, even though they knew that to do so would probably just get them killed. That was exactly what was going to happen in about a minute unless Whitaker had the sense to surrender, Hank thought. He settled the sights of his rifle on Whitaker's chest. Whatever happened, the outlaw leader would go down.

Slowly, Whitaker began to raise his hands. "Reckon you've got us penned in," he said with a shrug. The other members of the gang looked at him in surprise. Brian Parrish appeared positively flabbergasted that Whitaker would surrender. But the bandits soon followed Whitaker's lead, lifting their hands away from their guns.

The screen door of the store suddenly banged open. The stage driver stepped out onto the porch, a fierce look on his face. Furious, he glared at Whitaker and said, "Try to hold us up, will you?"

The guard grimaced and waved a hand at his partner. "Dammit, get back inside, you fool—" he started to say.

Whitaker's upraised right hand dropped and flashed toward his gun as the driver blocked the shotgun of the storekeeper, who was still crouched inside at the window.

Hank bit back a curse and squeezed the trigger of the Henry. It boomed and kicked against his shoulder, but he saw through the sudden haze of powdersmoke that Whitaker had used his other hand to grab the reins and jerk his horse to the side. Hank's bullet screamed past the outlaw leader, missing Whitaker by mere inches and splattering against the stone steps of the porch.

All the desperadoes had their guns out now. Whitaker's first shot took the driver in the chest, knocking him back in a sprawl that signified death. The shotgun guard came up out of his crouch and cut loose with the greener. One of the gang flew out of his saddle, his midsection torn almost in two by the load of buckshot. But before the guard could do anything else, he was flung backward off the box by the bullets that thudded into him. He landed on top of the team, and the gunfire-spooked horses lunged forward, throwing their weight against the brake, which gave with a sharp crack. The team plunged ahead, trampling the body of the fallen guard.

Hank shifted his aim and tried again for Whitaker as the gang threw lead into the store. The dust kicked up by the team made it hard for Hank to see what was happening, though, and once more his shot went wild. The boom of the Henry reminded a couple of the outlaws that he was up in the tree. They wheeled their horses around and started firing at him.

Bullets whined through the leaves around Hank, several of them slicing off twigs. He scuttled backward on the limb, scraping his free hand on the rough bark as he did so. A slug smacked into the trunk of the cypress just above his head.

He raised a leg, swung it over, and slid off the branch, letting himself drop the dozen feet to the ground. He landed hard, jarring every bone in his body. But to stay where he had been would have left him an easy target for the outlaws. As it was, he heard the angry hiss of bullets close to his head as he rolled desperately behind the trunk of the tree.

Hank stood up, trying to make himself as small as possible. More bullets thudded into the other side of the cypress. He could feel their impact clear through the trunk.

Somebody let out a yell, and hoofbeats pounded heavily. Whitaker and the gang were making a break for it, Hank supposed. He took a deep breath, then twisted around, bringing up the Henry and edging to the side enough to aim around the tree. Several of the outlaws had managed to turn their horses and were galloping back the way they had come. Hank's angle on them was a bad one, so he tried to hit some of the men whose horses were still dancing around wildly in front of the store.

Casebolt was firing from inside the building, and the deep-throated roar of the storekeeper's shotgun echoed along the shady banks of the creek. Hank fired as fast as he could work the lever of his rifle, peppering the gang with lead. He saw another man go flying out of his saddle to join the two who were already lying limp on the ground.

Whitaker and another man put the spurs to their horses and darted ahead, skirting the stagecoach, which had come to a halt again some twenty yards from the store. Hank threw a shot after them, realizing just as he squeezed the trigger that the other man was Brian Parrish. There was no time to worry about former friendships, though, especially when Brian had chosen to ride with a man like Whitaker. Hank grimaced in disgust as they pounded away. His bullet hadn't hit anything, and as he levered the Henry again he saw that it was empty.

Casebolt ran out onto the porch and fired after Whitaker and Parrish. The other outlaws were out of sight now, having taken off in the other direction—except for the three who had fallen. Casebolt turned the air blue with profanity as Whitaker and Parrish reached another bend in the creek—and safety. Suddenly, Parrish's horse stumbled, and the young outlaw clutched at his saddle. He was too late. He went sailing through the air to tumble with a splash into the shallow waters of the creek.

Out of the corner of his eye, Hank saw Parrish take his spill. He was sliding fresh .44 cartridges from his cartridge belt into the magazine of the Henry as Parrish came to his feet. "Isom!" Parrish called in desperation. His horse had regained its footing and kept running.

Whitaker reined in for a second and threw a glance over his shoulder at his fallen companion. Turning back again, he put the spurs to his mount and vanished around the bend of the creek.

Casebolt fired his rifle, the bullet kicking up a splash only a couple of feet from Parrish. The outlaw wasted a split second gaping back toward the store, then launched into a run that took him out of sight around the bend as well.

"I'll get him, Joe!" Hank called to his partner as he took off after Parrish. Casebolt waved a hand in acknowledgment, then dropped to a knee to check the condition of the stagecoach driver whose rash move had ruined their plan.

Hank's breath rasped in his throat as he ran after Brian Parrish. The Henry was fully loaded again and ready in his hands. The riding boots he wore weren't even made for walking, let alone running, but Hank did the best he could. Parrish wasn't in any better shape, he told himself.

But Brian had always been faster, Hank remembered. They had raced each other when they were kids, and Brian had nearly always won.

Blood pounded in Hank's head from the exertion. He reached the creek's bend and hurried around it, aware too late that he should have been more careful. Parrish could have been lying in wait for him. There was no sign of the outlaw, though. Hank plunged ahead, sticking to the creek bank. Parrish was probably doing the same thing; there wasn't much cover right around here once you got away from the stream.

Isom Whitaker was gone, nowhere in sight. A part of Hank's brain was bitterly aware that the outlaw leader had made a successful escape . . . again. Only this time it had been from a trap that should have been foolproof.

Hank glanced over his shoulder. He saw Casebolt about a quarter of a mile behind him, hurrying along in his wake. The situation back at the store must have been under control, Hank thought fleetingly, then returned his attention to what he was doing. There were enough cypress roots along the ground here so that one of them might trip him up if he wasn't careful.

He heard some crashing in the brush up ahead and knew that it must be Parrish. Hank slowed down a little. The undergrowth along the bank got thicker ahead of him, and it must have slowed Parrish down considerably. Hank looked over his shoulder again. Casebolt was still a good ways back, but Hank didn't think he would need any help now. He had the rifle and his own Colt against probably just one handgun, if Parrish had even managed to hold on to that much when his horse threw him.

The noise in the brush stopped, started again, stopped. Hank glided forward, the Henry leveled toward the area where the sound had come from. He passed a particularly thick-boled cypress and called out, "You might as well give up, Parrish. You can't get away."

A harshly drawn breath from behind him and to one side made Hank freeze. A ragged voice said, "I don't know how the hell you . . . you know my name, Ranger, but I'll kill you if you move."

Hank stayed still except for his head. He turned it slightly and cast his eyes around to see Brian Parrish leaning against the trunk of the big tree. Parrish still had his Colt, all right. The barrel was lined on Hank's head, and it was held in a rock-steady grip.

"Turn around slow," Parrish went on.

Hank did as he was told. He looked back down the creek. Casebolt was still a couple of hundred yards away, and from where he was, the older Ranger wouldn't be able to see Parrish. Casebolt had to be wondering why he had stopped short, Hank thought.

A stunned expression appeared on Parrish's features as he saw his captive's face. "Hell, I know you," he said. "You're Hank Littleton. You're a goddamn Ranger?"

"That's right," Hank said, trying to keep his voice calm. Maybe he could keep Parrish talking until Casebolt got close enough to know what was going on. "We've both come a long way from San Saba, Brian. Why don't you put that gun down and come on back to the store with me?"

Parrish shook his head. His wet hair was matted to his skull, and his eyes were wide with excitement and fear. "Can't do that," he said. "But you drop your guns and maybe I won't have to shoot you. I just want to get out of here, Hank. That's all I want."

"Sorry, Brian," Hank replied. He drew a deep breath. "I can't let you do that. You're under arrest."

It was a bold statement in a bad situation, and Hank knew it. There was no way he could turn the Henry's muzzle enough to get a shot off at Parrish before the outlaw could pull the trigger. And Parrish was just too damned close to him to miss. . . .

Hank saw the sudden urge to kill in the eyes of the man who had been his friend.

Something crashed out of the brush behind Hank, something that squalled and stunk and plowed right into him before Parrish could fire. The impact against Hank's left shoulder sent him spinning to the ground. Parrish let out a frightened yell as the thing lunged past him.

Hank's left shoulder was numb when he hit the ground, but he knew he had been given a chance. He lifted the Henry and fired it one-handed. The slug burned along Brian Parrish's forearm, making him drop his gun. He clutched at the bloody furrow and howled in pain as he staggered back against the tree.

Hank dropped the rifle and yanked his pistol from its holster. Earing back the hammer, he said, "Don't move, Parrish. I'll kill you next time."

Then he glanced toward the thing that had hit him, unable to keep his eyes off it any longer. It was the ugliest, most ungainly-looking creature he had ever seen, but it was running like the wind as it galloped along the bank of the creek. Fifty yards away, Casebolt had stopped in his tracks as it passed him and turned to watch it with the same fascination. The beast's ugly face, long neck, and humped back added up to the strangest thing either of the Rangers had ever seen.

"Goddamn it!" Casebolt yelled. "That there's a camel!"

Enough feeling had come back into Hank's left arm and shoulder for him to use it to brace himself as he climbed to his feet. He kept the Colt leveled at the wounded Parrish while Casebolt shook himself back to his senses and came jogging up to the two of them.

"I got this one, Joe," Hank told his partner, "with a little help from one of those critters you said wasn't around here any more."

Casebolt was still shaking his head in amazement. The camel had disappeared up the creek, returning to the concealment of the thick brush. "Wouldn't have believed it if'n I hadn't seen it with my own eyes," Casebolt muttered. "And that weren't even a very big one, probably not much more'n a baby. That means they're still breedin' out here in these hills!"

"We'll come back and catch it for you some other time," Hank said. He gestured at his prisoner with the barrel of the Colt. "Come on, Parrish, let's get back to the store."

Casebolt frowned. "You know this owlhoot?" he asked in surprise.

"It's a long story," Hank replied. "We'll go over that later, too."

"Any sign of Whitaker?"

Hank shook his head as Brian Parrish laughed harshly, humorlessly. "Whitaker's long gone," the young outlaw told them. "He's no fool. You won't ever catch him."

Casebolt grunted. "He don't appear to think overmuch of his pards, neither, the way he lit out when you went down, boy."

Parrish shook his head as he straightened up away from the tree. "Whitaker will be back for me," he claimed. "You'll see. And there won't be a damn thing you can do about it."

"We'll see, all right," Casebolt said. "Come on." As they started back toward the store, Parrish in front and the two Rangers trailing him, their guns drawn, Casebolt asked Hank, "You all right, son?"

Hank smiled grimly and flexed his sore shoulder. "Reckon I am, except for being trampled by a camel."

Casebolt had to shake his head again. "Damnedest thing I ever saw," he muttered. "Reckon we ought to make him an honorary Ranger?"

"Only if you pin the badge on him," Hank said.

Chapter Twelve

There were five dead men back at Camp Verde. Three outlaws had been killed in the brief battle, and so had the stagecoach driver and guard. The passengers from the coach, who had hugged the floor inside the store when the shooting started, and the storekeeper were all uninjured.

"Never figured that damn fool would run out like that," Casebolt said as he tied a rough bandage around the crease on Brian Parrish's arm. "I told ever'body just to stay put until them owlhoots had dropped their guns, but I reckon that feller just got too excited. Got hisself killed, and his partner, too."

Hank looked at the bodies of the three outlaws, which had been placed on the porch of the store. He couldn't put a name to any of them, but a couple of them looked vaguely familiar. Probably men who had ridden with Whitaker in the State Police, like Parrish, Hank thought.

It was a grim job, but Hank and the male passengers managed to hoist the five corpses up onto the roof of the coach. Casebolt kept a gun on Parrish while that chore was being performed. Hank finished tying down the bodies, then asked the passengers, "Any of you men able to drive a stagecoach?"

One of them nodded. "I reckon I can handle the rig. It'll be a little tricky going through the pass with a busted brake, but I think we can do it."

"You're elected then, mister," Casebolt told him. "The rest of you folks pile in and we'll head on to Bandera."

"Shouldn't you go back to Kerrsville?" the storekeeper asked. "We're still in Kerr County down here."

Casebolt shook his head. "Bandera's closer, and we're takin' the prisoner there. If the Kerr County sheriff's got any complaints, he can take 'em up with Cap'n McNelly." He jerked his head toward the coach. "Get on board, Parrish."

Parrish climbed in. His face was pale under its tan. The wound on his arm was bloody but not serious. He took a seat facing backward, next to the other man who had been traveling alone. Hank tied his horse to the back of the coach, along with Casebolt's mount, then swung up inside the vehicle while the older Ranger climbed onto the box with the man who had volunteered to drive. Quarters were pretty cramped inside, but somebody had to keep an eye on Parrish.

Besides, Hank sure as hell didn't want to ride on top with the dead men.

Hank settled down on the rear seat, opposite Parrish. The woman and the three children sat next to him, while the woman's husband took the remaining seat beside Parrish. The three kids were chattering excitedly, unfazed by the gun battle they had witnessed less than an hour earlier.

Leaning back against the hard wooden bench as the coach jerked into motion, Hank tried to find a position that would ease his aching muscles. The long wait in the tree, the fall from its branches, and the encounter with a stampeding baby camel had left him stiff and sore. The twelve miles to Bandera would be long ones, Hank knew.

And they would arrive with their mission only partially completed. Today's events had dealt a blow to Isom Whitaker's gang, but the outlaw leader was still on the loose. He would join up with his remaining men again, and it probably wouldn't be that difficult to find more hardcases to ride with the gang.

Hank looked across at Brian Parrish, who was staring sullenly down at the floor of the rocking, jolting coach.

* * *

Sam Knight was waiting for them as the coach rolled to a stop in front of the jail. A crowd had started to gather as soon as the coach reached the edge of town. The sight of the bodies tied on top of it had ensured plenty of attention from the citizens of Bandera. Following Casebolt's orders, the passenger who was handling the team had driven down Main Street and headed for the county offices rather than making the usual stop at the Riverside Inn.

Sheriff Knight looked up at the box as the coach came to a halt and said, "Looks like you had trouble, Joe."

"Reckon you could say that," Casebolt grunted. "There was a mite of shootin', and these fellers got killed." The Ranger hopped down from the box with an agility that belied his age.

"What about Whitaker?" Knight asked.

Casebolt shook his head. "Got away, dammit. But we got one of his pups." He opened the door of the coach and let the passengers climb out.

Hank and Parrish waited until the others had gotten out, then Hank gestured toward the door with the barrel of his Colt. "Don't reckon you'll try anything funny right here in the middle of town," he said, "but just in case you do . . ."

Parrish shook his head. "Don't worry, Hank. I'm not going to try anything. Why waste my time? Whitaker will be back for me later."

Hank just grunted and watched as Parrish hopped lithely down from the coach. There was a stir in the crowd at the sight of the captured outlaw with the bloody bandage on his arm. Knight and Casebolt moved in on either side of him, their guns out and ready. The sheriff said, "Come along, mister. We've got just the place for you."

"Might ought'a have the doc take a look at that arm of his 'fore you put him in jail," Casebolt suggested. "I patched it up best I could, but I ain't no sawbones."

"All right," Knight nodded. "We'll just pay a visit to the doctor's office first." He pointed to the bodies on top of the coach and said to the bystanders, "Some of you boys get those fellas on down to the undertaker's, and a couple of you take the Rangers' horses back to the stable."

Hank fell in behind Knight and Casebolt as they started through the crowd with the prisoner. The citizens of Bandera pulled back to form a passage, but they kept watching with avid interest. This was a day that would be talked about for a long time, Hank knew.

All the way back from Camp Verde, Brian Parrish had not said a word to him. Hank was grateful for that in a way. He had no doubts that he had done his duty by capturing Parrish, but it would have made things more difficult if Brian had spent the trip reminiscing about old times.

The crowd followed along as the lawmen took their prisoner to the doctor's office. While the medico cleaned and rebandaged the bullet crease on Parrish's arm, Hank waited on the porch outside and listened to the chatter of the crowd. Recognizing several of the men he had become acquainted with during his stay in Bandera, he nodded greetings to them, but the look on his face was enough to let anybody know he didn't feel like talking.

When Parrish's wound had been taken care of, Knight, Casebolt, and Hank took him back down to the jail. Knight went up the ladder first, then stood on the roof with his gun out while Parrish ascended awkwardly. Hank came up next, pulling the ladder up after him. The sheriff unlocked the trapdoor in the roof and flung it back. As Hank slid the ladder down through the opening, Parrish looked at it dubiously and said, "It's going to get mighty hot in there, Sheriff."

"It's not as bad as you'd think," Knight told him. "There's one window, and the walls are thick enough to keep some of the heat out. Anyway, you should've thought of things like that before you went around robbing stagecoaches. Now get on in there."

With an apprehensive look on his face, Parrish went down the ladder into the shadowy interior of the jail. Hank pulled up the ladder, and Knight closed the trapdoor with a shove of his foot. It banged down with a sound like a coffin closing, Hank thought. He had heard plenty of those, having grown up with an undertaker for a grandfather.

When Hank and Knight were back on the ground, the sheriff sighed and said, "Too bad it's not Whitaker we've got locked up in there. Why don't you boys come on back to the house with me? Faye and Victoria will be glad to feed you some supper, and you can tell me about what happened."

Casebolt nodded. "Sounds like a good idea to me."

"What about Parrish?" Hank asked, indicating the jail. "He'll need some supper, too."

"Don't worry about him, Hank," Knight said. "I'll bring something over for him later. I've never let a prisoner starve to death yet."

That answer satisfied Hank, and he fell in step beside Knight and Casebolt as the two older men started toward the sheriff's house. Knight reached up to wearily rub his neck, and Casebolt said, "You look plumb tuckered out, Sam."

"I haven't been sleeping too well here lately."

"Bein' a lawman don't rest very easy on some folks' heads," Casebolt agreed. "Especially them that's the worryin' kind to start with. Now, me, I try not to worry overmuch 'bout anything. I figger what gets took care of gets took care of, and there ain't much you can do about the other things."

Knight grinned. "I suppose that's the best way to look at it. Like Whitaker, you mean."

" 'Zactly. We'll catch him when we catch him. It don't do no good to agonize none over it."

The sheriff laughed. "You're right as rain, Joe. I—"

He stopped suddenly, making Hank nearly run into him. They had just turned off Main Street, and Knight was craning his neck to watch a woman who was driving past in a buggy. Hank followed the sheriff's gaze and saw a blonde in a fancy-looking traveling outfit that was dusty from long hours on the road. She handled the buggy with practiced ease as she drove down the street. Hank didn't remember having seen her around Bandera before.

Casebolt was watching her, too. She didn't appear to notice the attention the three men were giving her. An attractive woman in her mid-thirties, she was probably accustomed to interested looks anyway. The three lawmen watched her drive on down the street and then come to a stop in front of the Riverside Inn. She got out and tied up her horse and went into the hotel.

"Mighty nice-lookin' woman," Casebolt commented. "She new in town, Sam?"

Knight didn't seem to hear the question. A moment later, he gave a little shake of his head, as if he were trying to clear it of something. He said, "Not new in town, no, but I haven't seen her around in about a year. Never expected to see her here again, either. I figured she had pulled up stakes and found her a new life somewhere else, just like Russ.''

"You mean your brother?" Hank asked with a frown.

"That's right, son," Knight replied. "That woman is Susie Brewer. When she was here last, she did some singing in the saloons, dealt poker and faro in a few of them. But mainly she was my brother's ladyfriend. I reckon she knew as much about the holdups he was pulling as anybody, but I never found any evidence to justify arresting her. Like I said, after Russ got away, I never expected to see Susie again.''

"Well, don't that beat all?" Casebolt said. "Why do you reckon she's back here in Bandera now, Sam?"

The sheriff shook his head. "I don't know. But I don't figure it's for anything good." Again he shook himself slightly. "Come on, I promised you fellas some supper.''

The three of them started walking again, but Sam Knight was still deep in thought and distracted.

So was Hank. They were having enough trouble just dealing with Isom Whitaker and his gang, he mused. What would happen if a desperado like Russ Knight popped up to muddy the waters even more?

Hank had a bad feeling about that, and if it was bothering him this much, he wondered, then what the hell was it doing to Sam Knight?

Susie Brewer had never expected to be back in Bandera herself, but Denver had gotten a little too warm for her to stay there. She had left with two thousand dollars that had recently belonged to a rancher who knew all there was to know about cattle but who didn't have one damn idea what to do with a woman like her. She imagined he had been hopping mad when he discovered she was gone. The thought could still bring a smile to her face, even weeks later.

She had come down through New Mexico Territory on the stagecoach. There were always men willing to look out for a pretty young widow and make sure nothing happened to her. The lie quickly became second nature to her, as lies usually did. Winding up in Sweetwater, Texas, the impulse had suddenly hit her to buy a buggy and cut across the center of the state. It was foolish, she knew, but the desire to see the places where she had spent the happiest times of her life had been surprisingly strong. She would pay a visit to Bandera, then go on to San

Antonio. She could find some wealthy, gullible man there and come away with enough money to get her to the Gulf Coast and then on to New Orleans.

It was a good plan, she had thought, but she hadn't counted on the pangs she felt as she drove down Bandera's Main Street. Everything she saw reminded her of those days with Russ.

God, it had been good. Laughter and danger and the feeling of being truly alive . . . that was what Russ Knight had given her.

She would never forgive him for running out on her.

Chapter Thirteen

Faye Knight and her daughter, Victoria, showed more restraint than others in the crowd on Main Street. They didn't loudly demand to know what had happened at Camp Verde, and Hank supposed that was because they were used to the law business, being a sheriff's family and all. But still, they were curious.

"I heard that you have a new prisoner in the jail, Father," Victoria said as she and her mother set extra places at the table for Hank and Casebolt.

"That's right," Knight replied. "He's one of Whitaker's gang that our friends the Rangers captured. What did you say the boy's name is, Hank?"

"Brian Parrish," Hank said.

Victoria looked at him. "That doesn't sound like an outlaw's name," she commented. "And you say he's only a boy?"

"My age," Hank replied. "I reckon that's grown up."

"Yes, indeed," Victoria said, nodding and giving him that smile that always made him feel a little like she was making fun of him. "It certainly is."

Casebolt put in, "Parrish was old enough to ride with a skunk like Whitaker and be a part of them robberies and killin's."

Victoria made no reply to that. She retreated to the kitchen to get the ham that her mother had cooked that afternoon.

Over supper, Hank and Casebolt gave Knight the details of the trap they had laid at the Camp Verde store, telling him about the gun battle but leaving out any mention of the young camel and the part it had played.

"That setup should've worked," Knight declared.

"Sure should've," Casebolt agreed. "It would have if'n that stage-coach driver'd had the sense God give a piss-ant—beg pardon, ladies—but we just did the best we could once things started fallin' apart. It's lucky there weren't more folks hurt."

Knight grunted. "I reckon five dead men is enough."

Faye paled and put down her knife and fork. "Five men were killed?" she asked quietly.

"That's right, ma'am," Casebolt told her. "Three of the owlhoots and the driver and guard from the stage. It was purty tragical, all right."

"It certainly sounds like it. Was the man injured whom you captured?"

"Yes'm. Hank there put a pretty good bullet crease on his right arm. That's all, though. Parrish'll live to hang, that's for sure."

Faye and Victoria both looked disturbed, and Knight said hurriedly, "That'll be up to a judge and jury."

Casebolt looked sheepish, aware that his comments had bothered the women. Hank thought he would have tried to put things a little more delicately, himself. Even living with a lawman like they did, Faye and Victoria probably weren't used to such talk at the dinner table.

When the meal was finished, Sam Knight pushed back from the table and said quietly to his wife, "If you'll fix up a tray for the prisoner, Faye, I'll take it on down there to him."

"Of course," she murmured. She and Victoria went into the kitchen, and Victoria came back a few minutes later carrying a wooden tray with a cloth over the food. She said, "I don't mind taking this down to the jail, Father. I know you've been tired lately. Maybe you should just rest and talk to Mr. Casebolt and Mr. Littleton."

Knight put his hands on the arms of the rocking chair where he had sat down and started to push himself to his feet. "You can't do that by yourself, Victoria, and you know it," he said. "It's my job . . ."

Hank spoke up without thinking. "I'd be glad to walk down to the jail and take the food in to Parrish, Sheriff." He saw the smile on Victoria Knight's face at his words and felt a surge of warmth. She must have liked the idea, too.

He hadn't talked to Victoria alone since the night he had kissed her on the front porch. He wondered if she had thought as much about that night as he had since then.

Casebolt was sitting in one of the armchairs and rolling a cigarette. He said, "Sounds like a good idea to me, Sam. Let the young'uns handle this chore, so's us old folks can rest up a mite."

Knight shrugged and settled back in his chair. "I reckon it'd be all right," he said. He looked up at Hank. "Just be sure you're careful how you handle that prisoner, son. He may be convinced that Whitaker's going to come back and bust him out, but I don't think he'd pass up an opportunity to escape if he saw one."

Hank shook his head. "No, sir. I don't think he would, either."

He took his hat down from the hook where it was hanging and opened the door for Victoria. As they went out, Hank heard Sheriff Knight saying, "Now, Joe, I'm not sure I'm ready yet to be called old folks. . . ."

Darkness had fallen, bringing with it a cool breeze that felt good after the heat of the day. Hank and Victoria strolled down the walk in front of the sheriff's house and then turned toward Main Street. As they did so, Hank said, "Why don't you let me carry that tray, Miss Victoria?"

"I don't mind carrying it," she said, but he reached out and took it anyway. After a moment, she went on, "Is this prisoner really as dangerous as my father made it sound?"

"Parrish has been riding with Whitaker for quite a while now. I reckon he's picked up Whitaker's ways, too. I'd say he's every bit as dangerous as your father made out, Miss Victoria."

"But he's unarmed and wounded, isn't he? How could he pose a threat to anyone?"

"You've heard about wounded mountain lions and how dangerous they are, haven't you?" Hank asked her. "Well, I reckon Brian is about the same way right now."

She paused and looked sharply at him. "Brian? You sound like you know him, Hank."

He grimaced and then took a deep breath. He had kept quiet about his past friendship with Parrish, not saying anything about it to anyone except Casebolt. And Parrish himself certainly hadn't mentioned it. He had been too sullen ever since his capture to say much of anything. But now Victoria's quick wits had caught him out, and he had to decide how much to tell her.

"I do know him," Hank finally said. "Knew him when we were both boys up in San Saba. But then he joined up with the State Police, and that's where he met Whitaker. From what I can tell, they've been riding together ever since. I'd wager that Parrish has been in on all the jobs Whitaker has pulled, was I a betting man."

Victoria looked up at him. Hank wished he could see her features better in the shadows. Finally, she said, "It must have been hard, putting an old friend in jail."

"He was my friend before he took up being an outlaw," Hank said, hoping he didn't sound too pompous. "That fella in jail is just somebody that I used to know."

"Well, he has to eat, either way," Victoria said. She started walking toward the jail again.

The ladder had been taken down and was lying against the side of the blocky building. Hank gave the tray back to Victoria and set up the ladder, then took the food again.

"How are you going to climb up there and carry that tray at the same time?" she asked.

"Shouldn't be too hard," he assured her. But he found that it was more awkward than he had expected, having only one hand free to pull himself up the rungs of the ladder. With his sore muscles from the day's exertions, it was even trickier. He finally managed to reach the flat roof, though, and set the supper tray down close to the trapdoor.

Sheriff Knight had given him a key, which Hank used to unlock the trapdoor. Lifting the heavy panel, he called down into the darkness, "It's Littleton, Parrish. I've brought you your supper."

"Didn't know Rangers went in for waitressing jobs, too," Parrish replied, his tone mocking as it floated up out of the deep gloom inside the building. "What are you going to do, chunk it through the hole at me?"

"Just hold on," Hank said, trying to control the anger he felt at the way life sometimes turned out. "I'll put the ladder down, and you can come up to get the tray." He straightened from his crouch beside the door and turned toward the edge of the roof.

He stopped short. Victoria Knight stood there, her slender figure clearly revealed in the moonlight.

"What the hell are you doing up here?" The exclamation was jolted out of Hank. "I thought you'd stay down on the ground."

"I'm curious," she replied simply. "I want to see the prisoner."

Hank was dumbfounded. Before he could gather his wits enough to say anything, Parrish called out sharply, "Hey, is that a gal I hear up there? Maybe you really did bring a waitress along, Hank!"

Hank took a deep breath. He strode across the roof until he was only a foot or so away from Victoria. Looking sternly down at her, he said, "You know good and well you can't stay up here. Your father told you how dangerous this fella is, and so did I." His exasperation got the best of him. "Why the devil would you want to see a killer and an owlhoot, anyway?"

Victoria's chin lifted in defiance. "My father has always tried to shield me from his work, Hank. I'm tired of it, and I won't have you doing the same thing. Just say that I'm curious, if you have to have a reason."

He shook his head. "I'm not putting that ladder down in that hole until you're back on the ground," he said.

As Victoria stared at him, Parrish said, "I'm getting mighty hungry down here, Hank. Why don't you just send the girl down with the food?"

"Well?" Hank demanded. "Is that what you want?"

He thought he saw a small shudder go through Victoria's frame. "No, I don't want to go down in that hole," she said. "But there's no reason you can't let Mr. Parrish come up to get the tray while I'm here. I'll stay right here, clean across the roof, and you can stand beside me with your gun out. He's not going to try anything."

She was probably right, Hank knew. Parrish wasn't stupid enough to jump right into the barrel of a loaded pistol. But he was damned if he understood why Victoria even wanted to be up here. Just as he was damned sure that he could be every bit as stubborn as she was being.

He gave an abrupt shake of his head. Stubbornness wasn't going to accomplish anything. If she had her heart set on getting a look at the prisoner, he wasn't going to stop her. But he was going to keep her safe.

"You get all the way over next to the edge," he told her. "And don't you move from there, either."

"You give orders like I'm one of your Rangers," she snapped. But he noticed that she did as he told her.

Hank pulled the ladder up, carried it over to the trapdoor, and slid it through. Then he backed away quickly, drawing his Colt as he did so. "All right, Parrish," he called. "Come on up and get your food. It's right by the opening, so you won't have to come all the way out. You try to and I'll put a bullet in you."

"Sure, Hank, whatever you say," came the answer.

Hank stood close beside Victoria, the muzzle of the pistol leveled at the opening in the roof, as Parrish clambered up the ladder. His head emerged, then his shoulders, and he stopped.

There was plenty of moonlight for Hank to see the grin on the handsome, bearded face. Parrish watched them for a moment, then said, "That's a mighty pretty girl you've got with you, Hank. Sure you don't want to send her down here to keep me company for a while?" His voice was a mixture of charm and arrogance.

Hank found his free arm sliding around Victoria's shoulders. Unsure why he had made such a bold gesture, he said, "You just pick up your food and head back down that ladder, Parrish. This young lady is none of your concern."

Parrish shrugged and reached over to pick up the tray. He used his left hand to balance it. "Sure, Hank," he said. "Say, ma'am, did Ranger Littleton tell you that him and me used to be good friends?"

Tentatively, Victoria began, "He said something—"

"That was a long time ago, mister," Hank cut in curtly. "Everything's different now, isn't it?"

"I reckon so . . . at least as long as you're holding that gun." Parrish's grin widened. "Who knows how it'd turn out if you weren't?"

Carefully, he started back down the ladder. Hank stood and waited until he was sure that Parrish had reached the bottom. Suddenly, he realized that his arm was still around Victoria's shoulders. The girl hadn't pulled away from him, but she was holding herself rather stiffly.

Hank pulled his arm away, hoping he hadn't offended her.

He went over to the trapdoor and reached down to grasp the top rung of the ladder, being careful to stand back so that Parrish couldn't throw anything at him from below. He pulled the ladder up, then took it to the side of the building. Returning to the opening, he closed and locked the door.

"Well, you saw the prisoner," he said to Victoria as he stood up. "What did you think?"

For a moment, she didn't say anything. Then, "He didn't seem like a killer to me. He might have robbed some people, but I don't think he would hurt anyone."

"That's where you're wrong. He was shooting like everybody else up there at Camp Verde. Could have been one of his bullets that killed the stagecoach driver or the guard."

"You don't know that." Her voice sounded faintly accusing.

Hank shrugged. "Nope. I don't. But I know the kind of men he was riding with. All of them were killers, and I reckon Parrish has the same stripes."

"You're awfully sure of yourself. I suppose that comes with wearing a badge."

Hank made no reply to that, ignoring the challenge in her tone. He nodded toward the ladder and said, "We'd better go."

Victoria sighed. "I suppose we should. Father might start worrying otherwise."

That made sense to Hank, but he was afraid Victoria wouldn't be able to understand why. She was an intelligent, strong-willed young lady, the kind who would want to do something just because somebody else told her she shouldn't or couldn't.

It was an infuriating quality, Hank thought as he followed her down the ladder. But he couldn't deny that it was an attractive one in some ways, too. . . .

They met Casebolt on the way back to Sheriff Knight's house. Hank saw the red glow of the older Ranger's quirly as he approached. Casebolt paused and nodded to them. "Evenin', youngsters," he said, as if he had not seen them just half an hour earlier. "Any trouble with Parrish?"

Glancing over at Victoria for a second, Hank hesitated and then said,

"No. No trouble with Parrish." He wasn't going to say anything about Victoria's insistence that she be allowed to see the prisoner. That was over and done with, and no harm had come of it.

"That's good," Casebolt nodded. "Your pa said he'd get the tray from the jail in the mornin', missy, so there's no need for you or your ma to worry 'bout it tonight."

"Thank you, Mr. Casebolt," Victoria said. "Are you going back to the hotel so soon? I thought you and Father would probably be chewing the fat for quite a while yet."

Casebolt grinned. "Chewin' the fat, is it? What kind of a way is that for a proper young lady to talk?"

Victoria returned the grin. "Whoever said I was a proper young lady? Certainly not Mr. Littleton here, considering that night on the porch a few days ago. . . ."

"Now hold on," Hank began, feeling an embarrassed flush heating up his face.

Casebolt held up both hands in mock surrender. "Don't reckon I want to hear 'bout any of that," he chuckled. "You younkers got your own concerns, and they ain't none of mine. I figger I'll take me a pasear over to Gersdorff's and get me a drink. Want to come along, Hank?"

"Maybe after I've walked Miss Victoria on home."

"I'm perfectly capable of getting home alone, if you want to go on, Mr. Littleton," Victoria said. "Don't concern yourself with me."

"I said I'd walk you home," Hank replied, taking her arm. "That's what I intend to do. How would it look to your father if you came home alone at this time of night?"

"Oh, Sam ain't there," Casebolt put in. "Said he had a errand he needed to take care of. Maybe you better let Hank walk with you, Miss Victoria. You never know when Whitaker or some other desperado might be lurkin' around."

"All right," Victoria said with a sigh, but she didn't sound too put out by it, Hank thought. "Good night, Mr. Casebolt."

"Night, missy." Casebolt strolled on toward downtown, turning to call over his shoulder, "See you at Gersdorff's, Hank."

"We'd better go," Victoria said in a low voice. "You don't want to keep your partner waiting."

"Joe won't mind," Hank said as he fell in beside her. "Give him a beer and a card game and a little piano music, and he's happy."

Victoria nodded. "And what does it take to make you happy, Hank Littleton?"

The question was unexpected, and he had no idea how to answer it. "I'm not sure," he finally said. "Knowing that I did a good job, maybe."

"There ought to be more to life than that."

And feeling the warmth of her arm where it was linked with his, Hank knew that she was right.

Colonel Duffy had remembered her, and there was a slight look of disdain on his face as she checked into the hotel. But her money was as good as anyone's, Susie Brewer knew, even if some people around here thought of her as little more than a saloon girl and an outlaw's mistress.

If she had wanted to take the time, she could have proved them all wrong, she knew. She had learned a great deal since Russ Knight deserted her. She knew how to take care of herself now, knew that someday she would actually be the fine lady she had always aspired to be.

In the meantime, there was nothing keeping her from acting like she had already achieved that goal.

She came down to the hotel dining room for a late dinner wearing a dress of fine blue silk with plenty of white lace around the neck and the sleeves. A silver pendant, a gift from a cattle buyer in Newton, Kansas, rested on her fair skin just below the soft hollow of her throat. Her blond hair was curled in the latest style, and all in all she looked as if she would be right at home in New Orleans.

Colonel Duffy greeted her as she entered the dining room, and she could see that there was more respect in his eyes now. Earlier, when she had checked into the hotel, she had been riding in the buggy all day and had not had a chance to make herself presentable. It was amazing what a difference a few hours could make.

There were only four other people in the dining room, two couples who had the look of travelers. Susie could feel the admiring glances of the men and knew without even looking that their wives were probably glaring at her.

That was a good feeling, she thought smugly.

She sat down at one of the tables and the Colonel's daughter, who served as the waitress for the dining room, came over to take her order. Not that there was much choice, Susie discovered. The girl said, "I'm sorry, Miss Brewer, but there's not much left in the kitchen. We've got some Irish stew and a little cornbread, but that's all. Oh, and one piece of pecan pie, I think."

Susie started to grimace, then put a smile on her face to conceal her displeasure. She didn't want anyone in Bandera to see her at less than her best now. "That will be fine, dear," she told the girl sweetly.

"Thank you, ma'am." The girl hurried away toward the kitchen, and Susie leaned back in her chair to enjoy the respect she had heard in the voice of the waitress.

There was a heavy footstep behind her, and for a moment Susie felt a surge of fear, a half-remembered reaction from the time she and Russ had been together. For all their passion, they had always known that someday the law might catch up to them.

But all that was behind her now. Forcing down the nervousness she felt, Susie looked up slowly and saw that it was indeed the law who had walked over to her table. Sheriff Sam Knight stood there, looking as big and solid as ever, his hat clutched in his hands. There was a grim expression on his face, and his eyes were cold.

"Miss Brewer," he said by way of greeting. He nodded.

"Sheriff Knight," Susie responded in kind. "What can I do for you?"

Knight gestured toward the empty chair across the table. "Mind if I sit down?" he asked.

Susie's lips curved in a smile. "Are you sure you want to be seen associating with a wicked woman like me, Sheriff?"

"I'll risk it," Knight said. He pulled out the chair and sat down. "I never expected to see you around here again, Miss Brewer. You mind telling me why you've come back to Bandera?"

"Would you believe me if I said I was just passing through, Sheriff?"

Knight shook his head. "No, ma'am, I don't reckon I would."

She gave a throaty laugh and said, "Then what's the use? That is the truth, Sheriff; I'm on my way to San Antonio and after that who knows? But I thought I would travel by way of Bandera and do a little reminiscing."

"About the days when you and my brother were running wild around here?"

"Exactly." Susie's reply was soft, but there was steel underneath it. "They were good old days, weren't they, Sheriff?"

"Not particularly." He sighed. "Did Russ put you up to this? He trying to get back at me?"

There was genuine surprise on her face and in her tone as she said, "Russ? I haven't even seen that son-of-a-bitch in over a year!" The reaction had been too strong for her to suppress, but as soon as the words were out, she smiled again and went on, "I'm sorry, Sheriff. I suppose under the circumstances that would be insulting you, too, and I don't mean to do that."

Knight's forehead creased in a frown. "Russ isn't with you?"

Susie shook her head. "Like I told you, I haven't seen him. After that gunfight with you up in Bandera Pass, I imagine he took off and kept running."

"What do you know about that?" Knight asked sharply.

"What everyone else around here does. You came back with a shot-up arm and no Russ Knight. Does that gall you, Sheriff? Knowing that you not only let an outlaw escape but that he was your own brother? It would bother me."

"Beg pardon, ma'am, but I didn't think anything would bother you. Not the way you ran with that snake of a brother of mine." Knight drew a deep breath as he saw the shocked look appear on Susie's face again. This time, though, it was accompanied by anger. He held up his hands, palms out, and went on, "Sorry. I apologize, ma'am. If you're really just passing through, I've got no call to insult you. You're a lady, I reckon, and you're entitled to respect."

"Thank you, Sheriff," she said stiffly. "Now, if you're through questioning me, I'd like to get on with my supper." Susie looked over Knight's shoulder and saw Colonel Duffy's daughter waiting just inside the kitchen door to bring her the meal.

Knight scraped back his chair. "All right, ma'am," he said heavily. "I'll leave you to it."

"Sheriff . . . you don't believe me, do you? About my just passing through, I mean."

"No offense, Miss Brewer, but I don't reckon I do. I think you and my brother are up to something, and I'm going to keep my eye on you until I find out what it is."

"Well, good luck, Sheriff. You're going to need it. And it would be all right with me if I never saw your brother again. I would suspect that you must feel the same way, after being humiliated the way you were."

Knight stared at her intently for a moment, his face tight with anger, then turned and stalked out without making any reply.

She had forgotten what a stuffed shirt Sam Knight was, Susie thought. For a moment, she almost wished that Russ was with her and that they were up to something, just to see how put out the sheriff would be about it.

But only for a moment. Then the girl brought the food, and Susie had to concentrate on finding a ladylike way to eat Irish stew and cornbread.

Chapter Fourteen

The circuit judge was due by in a week, so until then Brian Parrish would have to stay in the jail. That was all right with Hank and Casebolt. Despite the fact that they thought it unlikely, there was always a possibility that Whitaker would try to bust his lieutenant out.

If that happened, they would be ready for him.

With the help of Sam Knight and several of the local men whom he deputized, the Rangers saw to it that someone was always watching the jail, usually from the porch of the county office building next door.

"We don't have to worry about Parrish getting out of there on his own," Knight assured them. "Nobody has ever broken out of that jail, and I don't reckon they ever will."

Hank and Casebolt were willing to spend a few days waiting for Whitaker to make a move, but if he didn't, they would have to get back on his trail. No reports had come in of Whitaker or the other members of his gang being spotted since the disastrous holdup attempt at Camp Verde.

Hank was grateful for the few days' lull. There were other things on his mind besides outlaws.

Like Victoria Knight . . .

He hadn't kissed her after walking her back to her house, but the thought had definitely crossed his mind. Victoria had seemed distracted about something, though, maybe the visit to the jail. He could understand how Parrish's suggestive comments might have upset her. So he didn't press the issue but just bid her good night instead and headed for Gersdorff's.

Over the next couple of days, Victoria was as pleasant as ever to him, but something seemed to have changed. She was distant, somehow, as if she was always thinking about something that he couldn't share. He and Casebolt took most of their meals at the sheriff's house, so Hank saw Victoria several times a day, but it just wasn't the same.

Three days after the shoot-out at Camp Verde, Hank was sitting on the porch of the county office building in the early evening, chair leaned back against the wall, booted feet propped on the porch railing, the Henry rifle lying across his lap. He had had supper an hour earlier, this time at the hotel, and was settling in for his turn at watching the jail.

He frowned and sat up as he spotted a female figure coming toward him in the gathering shadows. Victoria Knight walked up to the porch, carrying a tray like the one she had brought to Parrish three nights earlier.

"Hello, Hank," she said. "I've brought supper for the prisoner."

Hank frowned. "I figured Joe would do that. He's sort of taken over that chore."

"He came by the house to talk to my father, so I told him not to bother. I didn't mind bringing it down. It's a pretty evening, a nice time for a walk."

Hank glanced at the western sky. It was still streaked with red from the sun that had set a half-hour earlier, while to the east the heavens were already a deep blue dotted with stars. Victoria was right. It was a pretty evening.

He stood up and said, "I'll take the food to Parrish. You don't have to worry with that."

She turned and started toward the jail. "No, I'll do it. My father keeps a spare key for the trapdoor in his office. I'll get it and go up."

"Not likely," Hank said with a grin. "Can't have you up there by yourself with Parrish."

"He wouldn't dare bother me, not with you right here close by."

Hank was more serious as he answered, "You don't understand, Victoria. I reckon he'd do just about anything to get out of that jail—including hurting you. He's an outlaw, and he doesn't care about anyone except himself."

"I thought he used to be your friend," she challenged.

"Used to be is right." Hank stepped down from the porch and took the tray out of Victoria's hands before she could protest. "You run along home now."

For a long moment, she stared up at him, and he could see the anger on her face. Finally, she turned without saying a word and walked away. Even in the dusk, Hank could tell how stiff her back was.

He shook his head. She was mad at him because he wouldn't let her put herself in danger from a known robber and probable killer. Hank had never understood women that well to start with, but Victoria Knight was a pure puzzler.

Susie Brewer came downstairs in the Riverside Inn and found Otis Fields waiting for her in the lobby, just as she had expected. The portly, middle-aged man smiled broadly as she came up to him. "Good evening, Otis, dear," Susie said sweetly as she reached out to finger the lapel of his coat. "Did you miss me today?"

"I surely did," Fields replied effusively. He had bushy side whiskers, a full moustache, and a rapidly receding hairline. His suit was the best that San Antonio had to offer, and he looked like what he was: a prosperous small-town businessman who had worked hard for his success. That success had made his waistline expand along with the stagecoach franchise he owned. The line ran between San Angelo and San Antonio, with stops at all the smaller settlements in between. Its headquarters were in Bandera.

Three days earlier, she would have said that she would be long gone by now, in San Antonio or beyond. But when she had run into Otis Fields the morning she intended to leave, those plans had changed. He had been one of her many admirers when she sang in the local saloons, and he had made no secret of the fact that he was still attracted to her.

Plans were made to be changed, Susie had thought philosophically. Why go all the way to San Antonio to find a man who could finance her trip to New Orleans when there was a perfectly suitable candidate right here in Bandera? Fields had spent a couple of days courting her, having had lunch and dinner with her both days, then lunch today. And now they were about to enter the hotel dining room again.

Susie hoped that Fields would find something else to talk about besides his business. Knowing how much a man was worth was one thing; hearing all the details of how he had gotten that way was another. But Susie would tolerate it, whatever Fields wanted to talk about. Then later there would be a walk in the moonlight, sweaty fingers clasped around hers, a kiss . . .

So far she had been able to limit Fields to that much, but the time might come when she would have to allow him into her bed. It wasn't a pleasant prospect, but she could live with it. There would be no great scandal involved, since neither of them was married and her reputation was sullied to start with. And if it would get her the money she needed to travel on to New Orleans, going to bed with Fields would be worth it.

As she had feared, Fields launched into his usual speech during dinner, telling her all about the way he had built his business up from one broken-down mail coach into the thriving enterprise it was now. He laughed over the tales of his own cunning and put on an air of false modesty when he talked about the value of his holdings. Susie smiled and joined in the laughter, looked properly impressed at the stories of his determination and ambition.

God, he was such an utter fool.

A headache developed behind her eyes as the meal progressed, and the fumes from Fields's cigar didn't help matters. The brandy they sipped after dinner failed to ease the ache in her head, so finally she said, "I'm sorry, Otis, darling, but I'm just not feeling well this evening. Would you mind terribly if we didn't go for our little stroll tonight?"

Fields's crestfallen features showed that he minded a great deal, but he tried to cover it up. Putting on a hearty front, he said, "Of course not, my dear. I'm sorry you're feeling poorly. If there's anything I can do to assist you . . ."

Quickly, she shook her head. Comfort from Otis Fields was not something she needed tonight. "I believe I'll just go up to my room and retire early," she said. "Dinner was lovely, as usual. I thank you for it."

"Why, you're quite welcome. And I thank you for the pleasure of your company, dear lady." He scraped back his chair and stood up. "Here, let me help you."

Fields walked her into the lobby, but she stopped him when they came to the staircase. "I'll be fine," she told him. "You needn't accompany me to my room."

"I don't mind—"

"I know that, Otis. But it's not necessary." There was no one in the lobby at the moment, so she came up on her toes and brushed her lips across his. "Good night," she said, then hurried up the stairs before he could stop her.

Thank God she had been able to get away from him, Susie thought as she reached the second floor and went down the corridor toward her room. Her head was splitting. There was a small bottle of laudanum in her carpetbag that would take care of that, though.

She reached the door of her room and opened it, stepping in quickly and shutting it behind her. The room was in darkness for the most part, but enough light came in through the gauzy-curtained window for her to make out the furniture. She turned toward the dresser where a lamp sat, intending to light it. She never got the chance.

A dark shape suddenly moved in the shadows, and a lucifer was rasped into brilliant life, the glare from the match striking her eyes and making her flinch. "Who . . . ?" she gasped.

A man's hand held the match. Slowly, it moved, bringing the circle of wavering yellow light closer to his head. The glow revealed strong features and a black Stetson pushed back on dark hair that was touched with gray. There was a cocky grin on the man's weather-beaten face.

"Hello, Susie," the intruder said in a voice that was all too familiar to her. "Reckon you thought you'd never see me again."

Susie's hands flew to her mouth, stifling the scream that tried to rip from her throat. She stared at the man and listened to the blood pounding in her head.

For one heart-stopping instant, she had thought that Sheriff Sam Knight had invaded her room. But then she had seen the range clothes that managed to be flashy despite the trail dust on them, the ivory-handled Colt canted jauntily on his hip in a holster of oiled black leather, and most of all the arrogant smile that said here was a man who knew what he wanted and was willing to do whatever was necessary to take it as his due. . . .

"Russ?" Susie Brewer whispered in a choked voice.

He turned and lifted the chimney of the lamp, touching the match to the wick until it caught. The light grew as he turned back to her. He shook the match out, still grinning, and dropped it on the floor. "You're a sight for sore eyes, gal," he said as he moved closer to her. His hands reached out and his fingers dug into the soft flesh of her arms. Jerking her against him, he demanded, "Aren't you glad to see me?"

Then, before she could find the wits to answer, his mouth came down on hers, crushing her lips with heat and desire.

There was no mistaking it, she thought as she sagged against him. Russ Knight had come back to her.

Susie's body responded to his remembered touch, and she didn't struggle when he sank back on the bed with her in his arms. There was some awkwardness at first, but that was to be expected. After all, they had been apart for more than a year. But within moments, all the old fires had blazed up again and Susie was lost in his embrace.

Afterward, she contented herself for a few moments with snuggling next to him in the bed, but then she had to raise up on an elbow, look down at his face intently, and demand, "Where the hell have you been the last year, you bastard?"

A hearty laugh rolled out of Russ's mouth. "Ever been to Montana Territory, Susie?" he asked mockingly. "It's quite a place. There're gold strikes all over the place, and where there's a boom like that, there're plenty of easy pickings to be had, too. But I reckon I got to missing Texas. Had to ride back down this way for a spell."

"Missing me, too, I imagine."

He grinned up at her. "Of course."

Rage welled up in her. In the next instant, she was flailing out at him, cracking her open palm across his cheek again and again.

"You son-of-a-bitch!" she gasped. "If you missed me so damn much, why'd you run off and leave me?"

Russ twisted away from her angry blows and caught her wrists. Throwing her onto her back, he flung himself on top of her, pinning her

120

arms above her head so that she couldn't hit him again.

"Stop it, damn you!" he hissed. "You've got no right to judge me, you little slut! I didn't just get here. I've been watching you for a couple of days now, watching you play up to that fat townie. Reckon you intended to nick him for quite a wad, once he'd had his roll in the hay with you!"

"Nooo," Susie moaned. "It wasn't that way—"

"The hell it wasn't. I'm not blind, girl." Abruptly, Russ released her and rolled away. Picking up his shirt from where it lay on the floor, he took a tobacco pouch from the pocket. As he rolled a cigarette he kept his back to her, still breathing heavily from exertion and emotion. She saw that he was trying to calm himself down.

Finally, Susie said, "I'm sorry, Russ. I didn't know you'd be here. I didn't know where you were. For all I knew, you were dead." She sat up and massaged her bruised wrists where he had grabbed her. "I would have gone to Montana with you, you know."

He held a match to the quirly and took a deep drag, then said, "I know. I'm sorry, too. I would've come back for you if I could. That damn brother of mine shot me up pretty bad, though." Russ laughed harshly. "If Sam had known how bad I was hit, he wouldn't have let me ride out of that pass without following me. He'd have stayed on my trail. But he caught some lead, too. I reckon he decided he'd rather go back to that pretty wife and daughter of his than risk coming after me again."

"You're . . . all right now, aren't you?"

Russ turned to face her with that confident grin on his face. "Hell, a few bulletholes never bothered me that much. I was back on my feet in no time, and now I'm as good as I ever was." Without warning, his hand flickered out to the holster hanging on the bedpost. He snagged the Colt and had it lined and cocked in a fraction of a second. Susie drew back involuntarily. "Haven't lost it, have I?" he asked.

She had to shake her head. "No. You haven't lost it, Russ. But what are you planning to do now?"

"I'm going to take up right where I left off," he said, letting down the hammer of the Colt and sliding the gun back into the holster. "I never should've let Sam run me off in the first place. He doesn't know it yet, but this is my county now, not his."

A mixture of excitement and fear surged through Susie. She hesitated, then said, "I don't know if that's a good idea, Russ. There are two Texas Rangers in town. I've heard people talking about them—"

Russ shook his head. "I'm not worried about the Rangers. I've heard some talk since I got here, too. They're after somebody else. They won't have time to bother us. No, the only one we've got to worry about is Sam."

"He . . . he warned me that he was going to keep an eye on me while I was here. It's probably dangerous for you to be here."

"If I know that brother of mine, he's probably asleep with his own wife by this time of night. Clean living, that's what ol' Sam believes in." Russ's mocking laughter showed what he thought of that attitude.

Susie pulled up the sheet, clasping it around her nudity. She wasn't sure how Russ would react to what she had to tell him now.

"I wasn't planning to stay in Bandera, Russ. I was going to move on to San Antonio. I want to go to New Orleans eventually."

"That sounds good to me," he replied casually. "But you'll go with me, and we'll get there when I'm good and ready." He drew in a lungful of smoke, blew it out toward the ceiling. "That all right with you?"

She knew what the answer would be, what it had to be. "All right, Russ," she said. "Whatever you want."

And so much for her plans, she thought. Her efforts with Otis Fields had been so much wasted time, but she didn't care. Not now that Russ was back.

"That's right," he said. He began to pace back and forth. "Whatever I want. And what I want now is for you to keep seeing that fella Fields."

"What?" She stared at him in surprise.

He flashed a grin. "I recollect that he owns the stage line that comes through here from San Angelo. Lots of big ranches out that way. There's probably plenty of money on some of those coaches."

There was another surge of emotion inside Susie's breast, but this time it was anticipation. Russ Knight's recklessness was catching, and she had always been susceptible to it. She licked her lips and said slowly, "Plenty of money . . ."

And then they were both laughing. The good times, the wild times, were back.

Chapter Fifteen

Hank had seen plenty of wagons stuck in the mud. He had seen the way teams could pull and pull, but the thick, gooey stuff had hold of the wheels and was not about to let go. Now he felt sort of like a wagon wheel, he thought, one that had sunk to the hub in black mud.

They were never going to catch Isom Whitaker. No matter how hard he and Casebolt tried, the outlaw would just keep on giving them the slip.

It was late afternoon when the two Rangers rode back into Bandera. Both of them were tired after a day spent in the saddle. The day before, Whitaker and his men had been spotted by a farmer on the North Prong of the Medina. The man had ridden a mule into town to tell Sheriff Knight about seeing the group of hardcases cutting across his place. Hank and Casebolt had started back with the man before sunup, but though they had cut the sign of the gang, the tracks had petered out after several miles on the rocky ground. All day long, Hank and Casebolt had searched for fresh tracks, but there seemed none to be found.

Casebolt winced and rubbed his jaw as they rode down Main Street from the west. "Damn tooth's started hurtin' again," he complained.

"I got to get me some more of that lemon extract from Miz Knight."

"You should've got that thing pulled a couple of weeks ago while we were in San Antonio," Hank told him. He was in no mood to listen to Casebolt's grousing. He was tired and frustrated, and if their failure to catch Whitaker wasn't bad enough, he also had to contend with the outright hostility with which Victoria Knight had been treating him lately. She had been cool toward him ever since the night he refused to let her take Brian Parrish's supper to him. After that whatever interest she might have had in him had evaporated.

He was better off, Hank tried to tell himself. Women were just too damn changeable.

The sun was setting as they approached the jail. Casebolt glanced in that direction and grunted, "Looks like Whitaker's just goin' to let that boy rot in there. I was sure hopin' he'd come to us for a change. Reckon we couldn't be that lucky."

"Circuit judge'll be here in a day or two," Hank said. "If Whitaker is going to try to get Parrish out of there, it had better be soon." He frowned as his voice trailed off. Something seemed wrong about the jail, and as he looked closer, he could tell what it was. The ladder was not in its usual place, which was lying on the ground at the side of the building. Instead, he could see the tops of it sticking up at the rear of the roof.

Hank glanced around. The town was quiet. There were a few wagons and riders on the streets, several pedestrians on the boardwalks in front of the buildings. Everyone he could see looked calm, which made it highly unlikely that an escape attempt was being carried out. But all Hank's instincts told him that something wrong was going on.

"Why don't you go on over to the sheriff's and get something for that tooth?" he said to Casebolt. "I want to check on the prisoner."

"What for? He ain't goin' nowhere, not out of that blockhouse."

"Just to peacify my mind," Hank said. "I'll see you at the hotel in a little while."

Casebolt lifted a hand in farewell. "Sure, if that's what you want, son." He rode on down the street while Hank reined in.

There was no one on the porch of the county office building, Hank saw as he tied his horse at the hitch rack. There was probably someone inside the building, likely one of the deputies Knight had hired, but that wasn't good enough, Hank thought with another frown. There should be someone out here where a close eye could be kept on the jail.

He slid the Henry out of the saddle boot and carried it around to the rear of the jail. The ladder was there, all right. Hank paused at the foot of it and cocked his head to listen as he heard a murmur of voices. One of them was coming from inside the building; that would be Parrish. The other came floating down from the roof, and Hank stiffened as he recognized the soft tones.

Victoria!

He heard her laugh. She wasn't in any danger, then, at least not any immediate danger. Not sure what he was going to find, Hank started up the ladder, moving slowly and quietly so as not to give any warning.

When his head poked above the low parapet around the roof, he saw Victoria sitting beside the open trapdoor, her back to him. She was leaning over, looking down into the jail. Hank could make out what she was saying now.

". . . sure you didn't mean to do anything wrong, Brian. I know that once the judge gets here, he'll believe you, too. It's not your fault those men you were with decided to pull that robbery."

Muffled words came from inside the jail. Hank couldn't understand them, but he got the drift of Parrish's response from what Victoria said next.

"I . . . I just don't know." Her voice was solemn now. "I think Mr. Casebolt is an honest man. He won't lie about what he saw. But Hank . . . I'm just not sure. He hates you, Brian. He's liable to say anything."

Hank's mouth tightened in anger. He stepped off the ladder onto the roof and snapped, "He's even liable to want to know what the hell's going on here."

Victoria's head jerked around, and she sprang to her feet as she saw Hank stalking toward her. She turned to face him, his anger mirrored on her own features. Before he could say anything else, she accused, "I could ask you the same question, Hank Littleton! How dare you come sneaking around and spying on me!"

From inside the jail, Brian Parrish called, "Hank? That you up there, pard?"

Hank ignored the mocking question. He pointed toward the trapdoor with the barrel of the Henry and said, "I'm a Texas Ranger, and I'm here to check on a prisoner. You've got no right to be up here, Victoria, especially not alone."

"What's Brian going to do, jump out of there? The ladder's back there, there's no danger of him escaping."

"You're still taking too big a chance," Hank insisted. "Besides, how'd you get the key to open the door in the first place? It's supposed to be kept in your father's office."

Victoria sniffed, and a superior look came over her face. "I've been in my father's office before. I know where things are."

"So you went skulking in there when nobody was around and got the key, is that it?" Hank guessed. He took several steps closer to her, bringing him to within a couple of feet. For a moment she looked like she wanted to flinch, but then she stiffened and refused to give ground. Exasperated, he said, "Dammit, Victoria—"

Her hand flashed up, the palm cracking across his face. "You can't talk to me like that!" she blazed. "You're not my father! You're just some tin-plated lawman who wants to send an innocent man to jail—" She broke off as a sob wracked her slender body.

Hank stood there stunned as an angry voice shouted from below, "Leave her alone, Littleton! You've got no right to come barging in here and molest that girl!"

For a long moment, Hank stared at the crying girl and tried to sort out this lunacy that he had walked in on. Finally, he said to Victoria, "You've been sneaking up here right along, haven't you? Letting Parrish sweet talk you and convince you that he's just some poor innocent boy who happened to fall in with bad company. Well, it's not true. He's as bad an owlhoot as anybody else in Whitaker's gang!"

Victoria's tear-streaked face snapped up. "How do you know that?" she demanded. "How do you know he did any of the things you've accused him of? For all you know, he hadn't met any of those men until that day they rode into Camp Verde."

Hank took a deep breath. "Is that what he told you?"

"He told me the truth. And he told me you'd lie about it because you've been jealous of him for years. I didn't want to believe that, Hank, but I can see now that Brian was right. You're *still* jealous of him."

126

Hank felt dizzy. Victoria's attitude, on top of the wearying day he and Casebolt had spent, were just too much for him to cope with at the moment. He waved a hand at the ladder and said quietly, "You'd better go home, Victoria. Just give me the key back first."

"What are you going to do?" Her voice trembled slightly with anxiety. "Are you going to tell my father about this?"

"Reckon I ought to. But . . . I don't know."

Victoria stared intently at him for a moment, then reached into the pocket of her dress and brought out the key to the trapdoor. She flung it at him. It bounced off his chest and fell to the roof. He barely felt the impact.

Then she brushed past him, going to the ladder and descending without another look in his direction.

"Now look what you did, Hank," Parrish said, his voice echoing against the walls of his prison. "You went and got my gal so mad that she left without saying good-bye to me. How do you think I'm going to sleep tonight with that on my mind?"

Hank glared down at the dark opening in the roof, his hands tightening on the rifle. There was no telling what lies Parrish had filled Victoria's head with, he thought. It would save the state some time and expense if he just emptied the magazine of the Henry right down through that hole—

"I don't give a damn *how* you sleep," he muttered. He kicked the trapdoor shut and jammed the key into the lock. He gave it a savage twist and then straightened up. Killing Parrish was the easy way.

He would wait and see the son-of-a-bitch hang instead.

Hank was still upset about the whole matter the next day, but he wasn't any closer to deciding what to do about it. So far, he hadn't said anything to Sam Knight about finding his daughter up on the jail roof. The only action Hank had taken was to remind the deputy he found dozing in the county office building that he should have been outside on the porch where he could keep a closer eye on the jail.

For the life of him, Hank couldn't see how a smart girl like Victoria Knight could be taken in by Parrish's lies. But obviously, that was exactly what had happened, and now there was nothing he could do about it. He had passed Victoria on the street that morning, and her earlier coolness toward him had gotten even chillier.

That afternoon, Hank and Casebolt were sitting on the porch of the office trying to decide what course of action to follow in their assignment. They had sent a report on their activities so far to Captain McNelly a few days earlier, Hank's long letter having been added to the mail pouch when an eastbound stage passed through Bandera. So far there had been no reply from their commander, but it was a little too soon to expect one yet.

"I reckon the Cap'n'll leave us be for a while longer," the older Ranger mused as he and Hank stared with slitted eyes at the harsh sunlight in the street. " 'Course, sooner or later, he's goin' to need us to move on. Happen that's what he decides, I reckon Whitaker'll have a free hand around here for a spell. I'd sure hate to see that happen."

Hank shook his head. "The sheriff will catch up to Whitaker sooner or later if we don't."

"I ain't so sure about that," Casebolt said with pursed lips. "He's a good feller and ever'thin', don't get me wrong, but I ain't sure his heart's in his sheriffin' any more. I figger that shoot-out with his brother took more out'n him than he wants to let on."

"Could be." Hank shrugged. "I think he'd like to catch Whitaker, too, though."

"Reckon any lawman would." Casebolt had been leaning back in his chair, but as he spoke, he let the chair down and straightened up. Looking down the street, he muttered, "What the hell . . . ?"

Hank heard the pounding of hoofbeats and the rattle of wheels. As he looked down Main Street to the west, he saw a cloud of dust rising and knew a stagecoach was coming into town. But it was making a lot more racket and moving faster than the coaches normally did.

Both Rangers came up out of their chairs as the coach flashed past them, the driver still whipping his team. The careening vehicle headed on down the street, until finally coming to a sliding stop in front of the building where Otis Fields had the headquarters of his stage line. The driver flung himself off the box and vanished into the building while Hank and Casebolt started toward Fields's office.

The heavyset stage-line owner emerged from the building before Hank and Casebolt got there. He was followed by the driver, and now the Rangers could see that the man had a bloody gash on his forehead. Hank broke into a run.

The stage driver jerked the door of the coach open and helped a sobbing woman out. She was on the verge of hysterics, and as Hank came up beside the coach and glanced through the open door, he saw why.

There were three dead men inside.

Grimly, Hank studied the bloody forms and saw the bullet wounds that each man had received. One of the dead men wore town clothes, like the crying woman, and Hank guessed he might be her husband. The other two wore range outfits. A traveling cowboy and the shotgun guard, more than likely, Hank thought.

Casebolt came up behind him and said, "What the hell happened here, Fields? Holdup?"

"That's right," Fields gasped. "The stage was stopped between here and Medina." The middle-aged man was pale and seemed to be having trouble catching his breath. The carnage was having a definite effect on him—either that, or the loss in revenue this robbery might inflict.

Hank and Casebolt had been introduced to Fields in Gersdorff's Saloon one night not long after they came to Bandera. Neither Ranger had been overly impressed with the man. He might have been a good man at one time, but success had softened him. Now, the shock of this crime had hit him like a blow in his broad stomach.

"Where's Sheriff Knight?" Fields asked as he passed a shaking hand over his face.

Casebolt shook his head. "Don't rightly know. Haven't seen him around since this mornin'." He turned to the driver. "But we're Texas Rangers, son, so you can tell us what happened out there on the trail. From the looks of things, it must've been a whole gang that hit you."

Hank felt his pulse quicken. The same thought had occurred to Casebolt that had struck him. This might be the first blow in a new campaign waged by Isom Whitaker.

The driver shook his head. "It was one man," he said bluntly. "He came ridin' out into the trail and held a gun on us, told us to stand and deliver. Pidge there"—he gestured toward one of the dead men inside the coach—"didn't cotton to that idea. He tried to cut loose with his scattergun, but the outlaw was too fast. He shot Pidge down. I jumped to help him, and the bastard shot me, too. Creased me a good one and knocked me out. When I come to, I found the two passengers killed, too, and the lady havin' a fit. Can't say as I blame her."

"Did the bandit molest the woman?" Casebolt asked.

"Near as I can tell, he didn't. He was just after the money in the express box. It's gone, box and all."

Hank spoke up, pulling his eyes away from the gruesome scene inside the coach. "What money?"

Fields answered the question. "Several of the big ranchers out around San Angelo pooled the money they got for their herds and were sending it to the bank in San Antonio. There . . . there was quite a large amount on the stage."

"Who knew about that?" Hank asked sharply.

"Why . . . why, I did, of course. And Lowell and Pidge did, too, but not until they pulled out of San Angelo this morning."

Hank supposed Lowell was the driver. He turned to the man and said, "You didn't know anything about that money shipment until you took the reins?"

"Well, I reckon I knowed about it a few minutes before, but that's all. Mr. Fields here sent some special orders up there to San Angelo for us in a sealed-up enveloped. The agent at the station there give 'em to me just before we left, and I read them then."

"That's right," Fields confirmed. "That's exactly the way we arranged it. I didn't want word of this shipment leaking out." He paled even more. "My God, I'll probably be expected to make the loss good!"

"You say one feller did this?" Casebolt asked the driver, looking dubious.

"Damn right," Lowell snapped. "Say, you don't think I had anything to do with it?"

Casebolt shook his head. "Didn't say that. I don't reckon you'd chance givin' yourself a bullet crease on the head just to make it look good. No, son, I 'magine you're tellin' the truth. We was just expectin' to hear a different story. Like it was a gang of men who did this."

"Well, there was just one of 'em, but I reckon he was hell on wheels. After he shot us up, he cut the leaders on the team and hazed 'em off. We'd still be makin' damn slow time if I hadn't run across those animals and caught 'em again. I was able to rig up enough line to get them harnessed again and come on into town at a run.''

"Did you get a good look at the man who held you up?" Hank asked.

"Good enough. He wasn't wearin' no mask. He was a good-sized fella, around forty years old, I'd say. He had dark hair, and he didn't wear no beard nor moustache.'' The driver frowned. "There was something almighty familiar about him, but I just can't place—" He broke off suddenly and stared along the street, then grabbed for the pistol on his hip, howling, "Goddamn! There's the son-of-a-bitch now!"

Hank spun around, bringing up the Henry rifle he habitually carried, and followed the driver's line of sight. His finger tightened on the trigger, then froze as he saw who was coming toward them at a run.

Sheriff Sam Knight.

Casebolt saw the same thing, and his leathery hand darted out to close over the cylinder of the Dance Brothers revolver that Lowell had yanked out of his holster. "Hold on there!'' he rapped. "That's the sheriff!"

"Sheriff or not, he's the one who held us up and shot Pidge!" Lowell insisted.

Hank's mind was whirling. He had been sure that the driver would implicate Isom Whitaker and his gang in the story of the robbery and killings, but the man seemed certain there had been only one bandit. That was surprise enough, but for Lowell to then accuse Sam Knight of the atrocity—

There was only one answer, and it hit Hank with stunning force. He looked over at Casebolt and saw that the older Ranger had reached the same conclusion.

Knight was breathing heavily as he came up to them, his hand on the butt of his gun. "What the devil's going on?'' he wanted to know.

"There's been a robbery, Sheriff,'' Otis Fields said shakily. "My coach was held up!''

"And three men have been killed,'' Hank added.

"You're the one that done it!'' Lowell said to Knight. Casebolt was still hanging on to the driver's gun, or he might have tried to blaze away at the sheriff.

Knight frowned in confusion. "What kind of crazy talk is that?''

"This feller here says somebody who looks like you held up the stage," Casebolt told him. The Ranger's tone was meaningful.

Understanding dawned on Sam Knight, and Hank thought he had never seen a man look more miserable. The lawman turned to Lowell and gestured toward the bodies of the murdered men, saying, "The man who did this looked like me, did he?"

"The spittin' image," Lowell declared. " 'Cause it was you!"

"No, friend, it wasn't," Knight said in a voice so low Hank could barely hear him. "You're right about him looking like me, though. Folks never could tell us apart when we were growing up. I got in a mite of trouble from time to time because of that."

"See here, Sheriff, what are you talking about?" Fields asked. The stage-line owner mopped his flushed face with a handkerchief. "If you know who's responsible for this, I demand that you arrest him!"

"I'll do more than that," Knight promised. "You see, Mr. Fields, I swore that if he ever came back to this part of the country, I'd kill him." He looked at the bodies again and sighed heavily. "The man who did this was my brother, Russ."

Then he turned and walked away, leaving the crowd staring after him.

Chapter Sixteen

Sam Knight felt like someone had hit him in the belly with a sledgehammer. He had never been one to believe in omens and such, but the nightmares that had haunted him ever since the shoot-out with his brother in Bandera Pass had to have been a warning—a warning that Russ was going to come back someday. And when that happened, one of them would have to die. It was that simple.

Knight found his steps taking him toward the Riverside Inn.

She was there. She would tell him where to find Russ.

Colonel Duffy was behind the desk when the sheriff came into the lobby. He looked up and frowned when he saw the expression on Knight's face. "What's wrong, Sheriff?" he asked without preamble.

"Susie Brewer," Knight said flatly, ignoring the innkeeper's question. "What room is she in?"

"Second floor, front," Duffy replied. "I heard some commotion outside a little while ago, Sheriff. Has something happened?"

"It sure has, Colonel. All hell's going to break loose." Without saying anything else, Knight headed for the stairs, leaving a puzzled Duffy staring after him.

When he reached the door of Susie Brewer's room, he pounded on it with a hard fist. The door was jerked open a moment later, and the woman demanded, "What the hell—"

She stopped short as she saw who was standing there, and for an instant, Knight saw something flare in her eyes, something that confirmed what he had feared. Then she spotted the badge on his vest, and everything changed.

"He's back, isn't he?" Knight breathed. "For a second there, you thought I was him. Didn't you?" His voice was sharp, demanding.

Susie started to shake her head. "I don't know what you're talking about . . ."

Knight pushed into the room, bulling past her. His hand was on his gun as he glanced around, even though he knew that Russ wasn't here. Susie was alone. He turned to face her and saw how pale she was. "You know damn well what I'm talking about," he snapped. "That no-good owlhoot brother of mine has come back to Bandera County. You were planning to meet him here all along."

"You're insane!" Susie said. "I demand that you leave my room, Sheriff, unless you have some sort of warrant to search it or arrest me. I know my rights—"

Knight grabbed her arms. He trembled with the effort it took not to start shaking her like a dog shakes a rat. "You're a lying bitch!" he grated. "I've seen you around town, playing up to Otis Fields! You and Russ set this whole thing up, didn't you? You may not know it, but he murdered three men today when he held up that stage."

"No!" she exclaimed. "You're wrong! I—I don't know anything about this—"

Knight's calloused hand cracked across her face. She let out a soft little cry of pain. Suddenly, Knight released her and took a quick step back. Breathing heavily, he looked at the red mark on her cheek where he had slapped her. "I . . . I'm sorry, ma'am," he said in a choked voice. "I don't know . . . I didn't mean to . . ."

"Get out!" Susie cried. "Just leave me alone!"

Knight went to the door. He paused and looked back at her. "I really am sorry I did that," he said. "But if you are mixed up in this with Russ, then you're as guilty as he is. And I'll see you hang for it!"

With that, he went out and shut the door solidly.

A headache was pounding behind his eyes as he went downstairs and back out onto the street, paying no attention to the people he passed. For the first time in his career as a lawman, he had completely lost his composure up there in Susie Brewer's room.

He had wanted to kill her, to take that soft white neck in his hands and snap it like a dried-up twig.

Knight was suddenly aware that the sidewalk was blocked in front of him. He looked up and saw Hank Littleton and Joe Casebolt standing there, grim expressions on their faces. Casebolt said, "We'll help you track him down, Sam."

Knight forced a smile. "Thanks, Joe," he said. "But you and Hank have your own job to do."

"Sheriff, it's our job to catch outlaws, whoever they are," Hank said.

Knight shook his head. "I appreciate it, but this isn't just law business any more, fellas. This is personal now. I'll find Russ by myself—and then I'll kill him."

Or he'll kill me, Knight thought.

That was a chance he would have to take. His face set in stony lines, Sam Knight pushed past the two Rangers and headed for the stable where he kept his horse. It was time he got on Russ's trail, before it got too cold.

And cold or not, he would follow it to the end.

Hank didn't think he had ever seen an unhappier-looking man than Sam Knight over the next few days. Even Casebolt, whose tooth miseries had returned in full force, looked more optimistic than the sheriff.

Not that they saw much of Knight. For the time being, he had left Bandera in the hands of his deputies and the two Rangers. Over the objections of his wife and daughter, Knight spent most of his time in the saddle, trying to track down his renegade brother. His hearty demeanor had been replaced with a gaunt determination. When Knight rode back into Bandera in the evenings after a day of fruitless searching, he had the look of a man obsessed.

And when the reports starting coming in about Russ Knight's activities, it only became worse.

Russ struck in Hondo Canyon, in Pipe Creek, in the Sabinal Valley. He hit stagecoaches and freight wagons and general stores and unwary travelers. It was a spree of lawlessness nearly surpassing even that of the Whitaker gang. And nearly always, there was shooting. At the least sign of resistance, Russ started firing. Five more men were killed in less than a week.

It was eating Sam Knight alive, Hank thought. Somehow, Russ seemed to know where it was safe to strike. If Sam headed west, Russ pulled a holdup in the eastern part of the county, and vice versa. Hank had heard stories about twins who seemed to know what the other one was thinking, and although he had never put much stock in such yarns, that seemed to be what was happening now in Bandera County.

In the meantime, Isom Whitaker appeared to have dropped off the face of the earth.

The circuit judge came through, held a hearing on Brian Parrish's case, and ruled that the prisoner be held over for trial on charges of armed robbery and attempted murder. Hank testified at the hearing, along with Casebolt, and as he gave his version of the story, he was all too aware of Victoria Knight sitting in the makeshift courtroom and glaring at him. As far as he knew, she had not sneaked over to the jail to talk to Parrish since the evening he caught her on the roof, but he wouldn't have put it past her. She was one stubborn young lady.

A letter for Hank and Casebolt arrived on one of the stages from San Antonio, having been routed there from Austin. It was from Captain McNelly, and it ordered the two of them to stick with the Whitaker case until the end of the month, but no longer. If they had not captured the outlaw leader by then, or at least gotten a solid lead as to his whereabouts, they were to report back to Austin.

Reading between the lines, Hank sensed that McNelly was disappointed in them. He couldn't blame the captain for that; they'd had one minor success and a whole string of failures on this job.

Maybe he just wasn't cut out to be a Ranger.

Susie Brewer's heart was pounding in her chest as she wheeled the buggy around a bend in the trail. She was northeast of Bandera, in the rugged hills above the Medina River. Keeping the buggy on the trail was hard work, but it was the thought of seeing Russ again that had really caused her pulse to quicken.

The note that one of the kids in town had brought to her hotel room contained directions for how to find the place where Russ wanted to meet her. It had also warned her to make sure she wasn't followed.

Susie knew that Sam Knight had been keeping an eye on her whenever he was in town, just in case she might lead him to Russ, she supposed. But she had spent an hour wandering up and down the streets, browsing in the stores, before starting out here. She was convinced that Knight was not watching her this morning. There had been no sign of him on her back trail as she drove out here, either.

He was probably off on the other side of the county, Susie thought with a smile as she piloted the buggy around another turn in the trail. Russ had been running rings around his brother for a week.

The trail dipped down into the valley of a small creek that emptied into the Medina not far away. There was a clearing next to the stream, and as Susie's buggy entered it, a man on horseback emerged from the trees on the far side of the creek. Susie brought the buggy to a stop and called out excitedly, "Russ!"

He waded his horse across the creek and reined in next to the buggy. There was a broad smile on his face as he swung out of the saddle and then helped Susie down. Drawing her into his arms, his mouth came down on hers in a long, passionate kiss.

A minute later, he asked, "That damn brother of mine didn't follow you, did he?"

Susie shook her head. "No one followed me, Russ. I don't think the sheriff was anywhere around when I left town. He's out somewhere looking for you."

"Sam always was a fool," Russ laughed. "I reckon I got the brains in the family." He kissed Susie again, then said, "Have you been having any trouble at all?"

"Not really," she told him. "The sheriff came to see me after that first stagecoach job. He got pretty upset when I told him I hadn't seen you and didn't know where you were, but there wasn't really anything he could do about it. He certainly couldn't prove otherwise."

"And he never will," Russ growled. "Ol' Sam might as well give up right now, because he'll never catch me."

"I know that," Susie said, leaning up to kiss him briefly on the lips. "I know that, darling. Nobody can catch you, not even those Rangers."

"Damn right," he agreed.

Then he kissed her again, and for a while neither of them thought about sheriffs or Rangers or any kind of law at all.

Hank rode back into Bandera late that afternoon. He had made a swing up the Medina, talking to folks and seeing if anyone had spotted anything suspicious going on. Other than the holdups that Russ Knight had committed, though, the county seemed quiet. No one had seen hide nor hair of Whitaker and his bunch.

Time was running out, Hank thought. There were just a few more days left in the month. If there were no breaks between now and then, he and Casebolt would have to start back to Austin, leaving Parrish in the Bandera County jail and leaving the rest of the job undone as well.

But the time would come when justice would catch up to Whitaker, Hank told himself. If it wasn't here in Bandera, it would just be somewhere else.

He reined in when he reached the building next to the jail. Casebolt was sitting on the porch, a rifle across his knees and a hand cupping his sore jaw. The jaw had swollen steadily since the bad tooth had flared up again, and Casebolt's voice was thick as he asked, "Have any luck?"

Hank shook his head. "There's no sign of Whitaker anywhere. I reckon he's finally moved on, Joe."

"Maybe, maybe not," Casebolt mused. "You could take a dozen men and look for a month and not peek into ever' hole in this county, Hank. I got me a feelin' that Whitaker's still out there somewhere, just a-bidin' his time."

Hank stepped up onto the porch and leaned against the railing. "How's the tooth?"

"Plumb miserable," Casebolt answered, shaking his head and wincing. "Feels like it's swole up big as a punkin."

"Looks like it, too." A tired grin stretched across Hank's face. "Maybe since that lemon extract of Mrs. Knight's isn't doing any good this time, you ought to try another cure."

Casebolt snorted. "You got any ideas? I'm willin' to try anything."

"Well, a fella I once knew swore by this poultice he claimed to make out of possum piss. Said it'd cure most anything."

"You're funnin' me, boy," Casebolt glared. " 'Tain't polite to make sport of a man in such pain."

"Or you could make a compress out of the belly hair of a young camel," Hank went on. "Of course, you'd have to go out and find one first, but that shouldn't be too hard around here."

Hank was moving as he said it, heading on into the sheriff's office. Casebolt looked like he was clouding up to rain all over him. Hank ducked into the office and quickly shut the door behind him, before the older Ranger could explode.

Sam Knight wasn't in the office, which came as no surprise to Hank. The sheriff was either at home or off looking for his brother, Hank thought. He stretched some of the kinks out of his back that had come from his long ride that afternoon, then sat down behind the desk to flip idly through a stack of reward dodgers. The grin dropped off his face. Ragging Casebolt was good for a few minutes of entertainment, but it wasn't going to keep his mind off their problems for long. There was still the matter of Isom Whitaker, not to mention the depredations that Russ Knight had visited on the county. Hank wondered if he should get in touch with Captain McNelly and ask to be officially assigned to Russ Knight's case.

That wouldn't work, he decided. For one thing, Sam Knight would regard it as interference, and rightly so. He had made it plain that he intended to track down his brother himself. If a local lawman objected to the presence of the Rangers, they were supposed to withdraw.

Besides, why would Sam Knight want the help of two Rangers who couldn't even do their own job?

Hank shook off that bitter thought and got up. He stepped back outside and glanced over at Casebolt, saw that the older man was still frowning but seemed to be over some of his annoyance. Quietly, Hank asked, "Why don't you go get some supper, Joe? I'll keep an eye on the jail. Don't reckon Whitaker's going to try to get Parrish out anyway, not after this long a time."

"That's just when a feller like Whitaker'll fool ya, son," Casebolt replied. "Just when you think he ain't a threat no more, he'll pop up again." Casebolt stood and stretched. "Don't know how much I can eat with this tooth like it is, but I reckon I ought to give it a try. I'll be back in a little while."

"Take your time," Hank told him. "I'm not very hungry."

Casebolt nodded and waved, then ambled away down Main Street toward the hotel. The Rangers had stopped eating at Sheriff Knight's house for the most part; the atmosphere in the place had just been too strained.

Hank could understand why. It had to be hard on Faye and Victoria, watching the sheriff turn hard and cold as he had. There didn't seem to be anything anyone could do about it, though, not even Knight's family. Sam Knight was living for only one thing these days—a showdown with his brother.

And if that day ever came, Hank mused, he wondered if it wouldn't just make things worse, assuming that the sheriff came out on top.

What would it do to a man to have to kill his own brother?

Victoria Knight slipped through the streets of Bandera as night settled over the town. Even though she knew that no one was paying particular attention to her, she felt like everyone in the entire town was staring at her. Like they could read her mind and see the thoughts that were tormenting her.

She was trying to decide if she could bring herself to turn against everything she had been taught during her life. If she could betray her father, in the name of love . . .

Victoria took a deep breath and tried to slow her racing pulse. It wouldn't do her or Brian any good if she went into hysterics at the mere thought of helping him escape.

A month ago she would have laughed—or been insulted—at the very notion that she would help a prisoner escape from her father's jail.

But when her eyes had met those of Brian Parrish, that first day when the two Rangers had brought him back to Bandera and she was part of the crowd watching the excitement, Victoria had known right away that something totally unexpected had just happened. Unexpected and frightening and perhaps very wonderful. In her reading, she had encountered the concept of love at first sight, but never in her wildest flights of imagination had she thought that it could happen to her.

The sparkle she had seen in Brian Parrish's gaze and the quick smile on his face had changed Victoria's mind.

At first she had fought against the idea and tried to convince herself that the interest she had felt in Hank Littleton could grow into something more if she gave it a chance. She was lying to herself, though, and deep down she knew it. She knew she had to see the charming young prisoner again, to make sure she hadn't imagined the jolt of energy that had passed between them.

Hank had done everything in his power to prevent it. He was jealous of Brian, Victoria could tell that. He seemed to think that since he had kissed her, that gave him some sort of proprietary rights over her.

Sooner or later, Hank Littleton would find out how very wrong he was.

Victoria had found a way to talk to Brian, even if she couldn't see him through the trapdoor in the jail roof. Their conversations had convinced her that she had not been mistaken. He was just as interested in her as she was in him. He had told her about the difficult days when he was growing up on a hardscrabble central Texas farm, about having to fend for himself since an early age. And he had told her about falling in with a group of men who had turned out to be outlaws.

That wasn't his fault, Victoria had assured him. No one could blame him for having some sheer bad luck.

Hank could. Victoria realized that when he came up onto the roof and acted like he wanted to shoot her and Brian both. The Texas Ranger was crazy mad with jealousy, she thought. Just as Brian had told her, Hank would do or say anything to have him out of the way.

Hank had lied at the hearing, just as Victoria had known he would. And so Brian was still stuck in that awful jail, sitting there alone in the gloom day after day.

It was fortunate for both of them that Victoria had found the crack in the timber of the building's rear wall. It was maddening in a way, to be so close but not be able to touch one another, but at least they could tell each other all the things they wanted to share. Victoria had been there, kneeling in the deep shadows behind the jail, nearly every night since the hearing.

Two nights earlier, Brian had said, "You could still get a key to that trapdoor, couldn't you?"

That simple question was the beginning. Since then he had told her about the horrors he would face in prison, even if he was lucky enough not to hang. Over and over again, he had proclaimed his innocence to her. He had never come right out and asked her to help him escape, but she knew that was what he was leading up to.

She was going to save him the trouble, she abruptly decided as she walked toward the jail. Even her stride seemed suddenly more determined, more purposeful. She knew where the spare key was; Hank hadn't told anyone about her earlier visits with Brian, as far as she knew, and so the key should still be in the same place. If no one was inside the office, it would be a simple matter to slip in the building's rear door, get the key, and climb up to set Brian Parrish free.

And as Victoria Knight strode toward the jail, she knew that was exactly what she was going to do.

Chapter Seventeen

Victoria paused at the corner of the jail and peered around it, being careful not to reveal herself. Most of the time when Hank or Casebolt were guarding the jail, they stayed on the porch of the building next door. Victoria edged forward until she could see long legs and booted feet propped on the porch rail.

They belonged to Hank Littleton. Victoria drew back, closed her eyes, and felt like using some of the decidedly unladylike cuss words she had heard from the local cowboys.

Despite how she felt about Hank—and she had to admit that she wasn't even totally sure about *that*—she knew that he had keen hearing and that he wouldn't be dozing like some of the deputies often did. There was a good chance he would hear her if she tried to sneak through the back door and into her father's office.

Hank was going to ruin everything, even without knowing it.

The sound of voices made Victoria steal a look around the corner again. There was another man standing in front of the porch now, she saw. Hank had stood up and was talking to the newcomer. Victoria looked closer and saw that the second man was one of the deputies her father had hired. She strained her ears trying to hear what was being said.

"—be glad to do it," the deputy told Hank. "Your partner said he'd relieve me later. Said you'd likely be pretty wore out."

"That's true enough," Hank replied. "Well, if you're sure, Mr. Buchanan, I reckon some supper would taste pretty good." The young Ranger came down the steps to the street, unhitched his horse, then led the animal away as he walked slowly down the street. Victoria watched him go and thought about what she had just seen and heard. Obviously, Casebolt had sent the deputy to take over for Hank. Victoria knew the man. Ed Buchanan was middle-aged and not about to do a lick more work than he had to.

A smile slowly formed on Victoria's face as she watched the deputy sit down on the porch. Buchanan would be dozing in the chair in a matter of minutes.

She waited. It was difficult, knowing as she did that Brian Parrish was just on the other side of the timbered wall next to her, but she had to give Buchanan time to get good and asleep. When she was convinced that he was, she stole around to the rear of the jail.

Crouching next to the crack in the wall, Victoria hissed, "Brian!"

She heard the scuttle of his feet inside on the hard-packed earthen floor, then he replied, "Victoria?"

"Yes," she said, thrilling at the sound of his voice. "I've come to set you free, Brian."

There was a quick intake of breath from the prisoner. Then he said, "Thank you, darling. I knew you wouldn't let me down."

Victoria hesitated a moment before saying, "There's just one thing, Brian . . ."

"Anything, sweetheart. You know that."

"I realize that you can't take me with you now, but later, after the truth has come out and your name has been cleared, you have to promise to come back for me."

"Of course." Brian's words came in a fast, sincere whisper. "I wouldn't want to live without you, especially after what you're going to do for me tonight."

"All right, I'll go get the key. I'll be back in a few minutes, so you be ready."

"I will be," Brian promised her grimly. "One more thing, Victoria."

"What is it?"

"You'll have to get me a gun."

The words sent a cold feeling through her. She hadn't even thought about that, but Brian was right, of course. He wouldn't need a weapon tonight, but no man went unarmed out here by choice.

"There should be some pistols in my father's office," she said. "Will one of them be all right?"

"As long as it works and has some cartridges with it, that's all that matters, Victoria. Can you handle that?"

She took a deep breath. "Certainly. I'll be right back, Brian."

Victoria straightened and hurried over to the back door of the office building. She turned the knob slowly, then carefully eased the door open. It was seldom locked, and this night was no exception. Victoria slipped into the darkened hall inside.

There was a lantern burning inside the sheriff's office, and its light spilled through the open door into the hall. Victoria moved up the corridor, past the offices of the county clerk and the tax assessor and the chambers used by the circuit judge whenever he came through. She darted through the door into her father's office, aware that she would have to move fast. There was a window that looked out into the street, and anyone passing by could glance through it and spot her.

She could see the back of the deputy's head as he slumbered in the chair on the porch. Carefully, Victoria opened the center drawer of her father's desk. The spare key to the trapdoor was there, as it usually was, in a heap of other spare keys. Victoria snagged it and thrust it into a pocket of her dress.

Getting a gun was more difficult. She knew that her father kept the pistols he confiscated from drunken cowhands in a locked cabinet next to the rack where rifles and shotguns were chained. The key to the cabinet was probably among the ones in the drawer, but she didn't know which one it was.

The only thing she could do was start trying them until one worked.

Victoria gathered up a handful of the keys and turned to the cabinet. One by one, she slid each key into the lock and tried to turn it. Her frustration mounted by the second as the first group of keys proved to be futile. She snatched up some more from the desk drawer, being a little less careful now in her desire for speed.

The third one in this bunch clicked over in the lock.

Victoria heaved a sigh of relief and pulled the cabinet door open. There were probably a dozen pistols hung on hooks inside it. She recognized a pair of them as Remington .36s, and there was a box of .36 caliber cartridges in the bottom of the cabinet. Victoria grabbed both guns and the shells, dropping the box of ammunition in the same pocket as the trapdoor key as she turned toward the door of the office.

She glanced out the window as she passed it and saw that Buchanan was still dozing. There was no sign that he had heard her rummaging around in here. She went out quickly, carrying the heavy revolvers.

Leaving the guns on the ground at the back of the jail, Victoria slipped around to the side and got the ladder. She propped it against the back wall of the building and started up, the box of cartridges bumping against her leg as she climbed. Although it took her only seconds to reach the roof, it seemed much longer. But finally she was there, kneeling next to the trapdoor and fumbling with the key.

The lock snapped open, and Victoria used both hands to lift the door. She let it down gently so that it wouldn't thump, then leaned over and whispered to Brian, "I'll get the ladder."

"Hurry!" he urged her, and she could hear the nervousness in his voice. The nearness of freedom was affecting him, too, she thought.

Awkwardly, she pulled up the ladder and brought it over to the opening in the roof. As she let down one end of it, Brian took hold and guided it down. Then she heard him swarming up the rungs, and an instant later, his head appeared in the moonlight.

She expected him to take her into his arms for a hug and a kiss, but as soon as he cleared the trapdoor he threw himself to the side and pulled her down with him. "Stay low!" he hissed. "If anybody sees us, they're liable to start shooting!"

Victoria was surprised at the roughness with which he yanked her down, but she supposed he was right. She started to say, "I'll get the ladder—"

"I've got it," Brian snapped. "Where's the guns?"

"Down below," she told him as he hurriedly picked up the ladder and carried it back to the rear wall. He stayed crouched down as much as possible as he lowered it to the ground. Then, without another word, he swung over the parapet and started down the ladder.

Victoria hurried after him. He had already reached the ground by the time she began to climb down the ladder. She glanced over her shoulder and saw him pick up the Remingtons. He pulled back one of the hammers slightly and spun the cylinder, then glared up at her. "They're not loaded, dammit!" he said in a low voice.

Victoria paused on the ladder, halfway down, and said, "I've got a box of cartridges in my pocket—"

"Give them to me—*now!*"

His harsh tone made her frown, but she lifted the box of ammunition out of her pocket and dropped it down to him. Brian caught the box, tore it open, and began jamming cartridges into the revolvers.

Victoria hurried down the ladder and stepped off it beside him. He still hadn't kissed her. She knew he was in a hurry to get away from here, but surely one kiss wouldn't slow him down that much. After what she had done for him tonight, after all the tender words they had exchanged over the last couple of weeks—

He tucked one of the Remingtons behind his belt, then reached out for her. Instead of drawing her into an embrace, though, his hand clamped down on her arm and jerked roughly. "Come on," he snapped.

"But . . . I thought I wasn't going with you."

Brian Parrish glanced over at her, his face an arrangement of angles and shadows in the bright moonlight. Suddenly, Victoria felt as if she didn't know him at all, as if he was a stranger who was pulling on her and trying to take her somewhere she didn't want to go.

"You're going with me, all right," he growled. "Those goddamn Rangers won't shoot as long as you're with me. Now keep your damn mouth shut and come on!"

The knowledge that she had just made the worst mistake of her life slammed into Victoria Knight. She had believed this man. She had let herself be courted by a killer and a thief, and now she had helped him escape from the jail where he belonged. Her heart felt like it was going to pound right through her chest as she opened her mouth.

Parrish saw what was about to happen and lunged at her, trying to clap his hand over her mouth, but he was too late.

Victoria screamed, a shrill sound that knifed through the quiet Bandera night.

Joe Casebolt turned a corner and ambled along Main Street. He had gotten some supper at the hotel, then dropped in at Gersdorff's for a drink. The whiskey had made his tooth feel some better for a little while, but now the ache was coming back.

He reached up and rubbed his jaw, his palm rasping over the beard stubble there. Maybe Faye Knight had some other remedy he could try, since the lemon extract wasn't working any more. If Ed Buchanan was still all right to keep an eye on the jail for a while, Casebolt decided, he would go over to the sheriff's house and ask Faye if she knew of anything else that was good for a toothache.

Possum-piss poultices and camel's-hair compresses! Casebolt snorted as he remembered Hank's suggestions. The boy had all the makings of a damn good Ranger, but his sense of humor left a whole heap to be desired.

He had thought he might run into Hank at Gersdorff's, but the youngster hadn't come in before Casebolt left. Probably still over at the hotel getting his supper.

He'd always had a fine appetite when he was younger, Casebolt remembered. Seemed lately, though, that things didn't taste as good. It wasn't just his sore tooth causing it, either. He wouldn't admit it to Hank or McNelly or anybody else, but he was getting old. Slowing down a mite. One of these days soon, he was going to have to start thinking about retiring.

What the hell would he do, though? he asked himself. He had been a lawman and a scout and an Indian fighter for nigh onto fifty years. Sitting on a porch and watching the world go by and waiting for all the aches and pains to just get worse sure as hell wasn't the way he wanted to spend the rest of his life.

Casebolt glanced up, some instinct breaking into his reverie and warning him that something was wrong. He squinted as he looked up the street. A block away, he could see Buchanan sitting in the chair on the front porch of the building next to the jail. The deputy's head was down, resting on his chest.

"Hell's fire!" Casebolt muttered to himself as he stepped up his pace. "Can't nobody in this fool town stay awake?"

He had gone only a few steps when the scream ripped out from behind the jail.

Casebolt's hand darted to the gun on his hip. He drew the Colt without even thinking about it and broke into a run. "Buchanan!" he yelled as he pounded past the porch. "There's trouble!"

He saw the deputy come up out of his chair, sputtering and looking around wildly as he tried to throw off sleep. Buchanan wouldn't be a damn bit of good for a few minutes, Casebolt knew. Hank was probably still back at the hotel, and Lord knew where Sam Knight was. The screaming from behind the jail was abruptly cut off.

Whatever was going on back there, Casebolt would have to handle it by himself.

He rounded the corner of the blocky building and raced along its side. The moonlight was plenty bright enough to show him the two struggling figures. One was a woman, Casebolt realized, and the other was Brian Parrish.

"Hold it, Parrish!" Casebolt shouted. He leveled his pistol at the outlaw, but he couldn't shoot. The girl—he realized suddenly that it was Victoria Knight—was just too damned close to Parrish.

Parrish spun around to meet the new threat, and that distraction was enough to allow Victoria to tear herself out of his grip. She tried to run but tripped and fell after only a step. Still, that was enough to put her out of the line of fire.

Casebolt's pistol blasted at the same instant as Parrish fired the Remington in his hand. The Ranger felt a slug thud into his chest and knock him backward. Casebolt triggered another shot as he slumped to the ground. The whole middle of his body had gone numb, but he could still lift the Colt and pull the trigger.

Parrish started to reach for Victoria. Casebolt figured that he intended to take the girl with him to use as a hostage. His mind was working clearly despite the wound he had received. He fired again, sending a bullet screaming close by Parrish's head. The outlaw jerked away from Victoria, snapped one more shot at Casebolt that kicked up dirt a foot away from the Ranger, then turned and ran.

Gasping for breath, Casebolt tried to lift himself to his feet. He couldn't do it. His strength was flowing out of him like water. The gun slipped from his fingers as he fell again. He blinked and peered after Parrish as the outlaw vanished into the darkness.

Victoria was screaming again as Buchanan came running up. The gunfight had taken only seconds. Buchanan dropped to one knee beside Casebolt and said shakily, "Joe? You all right, Joe?"

"Not hardly, you ol' idiot!" Casebolt rasped. He waved a hand weakly as the sound of hoofbeats came to his ears. Parrish had already found a horse to steal. "That's Parrish," Casebolt went on. "He's gettin' away. . . . You'd best . . . fetch the sheriff . . . and find Hank—"

For a hot night, Casebolt thought as his head fell back, it sure was getting a mite chilly.

Hank heard the screams as he stepped out onto the porch of the hotel after his supper. They cut through the weariness that had gripped him. He bounded off the porch and started toward the jail. Maybe that wasn't where the trouble was, but he couldn't afford to take that chance.

He had dropped off the Henry in his room after putting up his horse. It was rare for him not to have the rifle with him, but he hadn't been expecting trouble tonight. Besides, he had been tired and hadn't felt like lugging it around.

Like Casebolt had told him, trouble had a habit of rearing up just when you weren't looking for it.

Gunshots shattered the night. Fear coursed through Hank's whole body, fear that something was terribly wrong. He could tell for sure now that the gunfire was coming from the vicinity of the jail.

Isom Whitaker had come for Parrish. That thought burned through Hank's brain.

The shooting stopped before Hank reached the jail. That wasn't a good sign. He ran harder and jerked his pistol out of its holster, and a moment later he rounded the corner of the jail, wondering where the deputy was.

Buchanan was kneeling beside a figure sprawled on the ground. A few yards away, a woman was also lying on the ground, sobs coming from behind the hands she had pressed to her face. Over the cries, Hank heard a horse galloping away in the distance.

Hank dropped into a crouch beside the man on the ground. It was Joe

Casebolt. There was a large dark stain on the front of Casebolt's shirt.

"Joe!" Hank said urgently. "What happened? Was it Whitaker?"

Casebolt's eyes had been closed, but they fluttered open at the sound of Hank's voice. The older Ranger gave a feeble shake of his head. "Not . . . Whitaker . . ." he rasped. "But Parrish . . . got away. . . . You'd best see to . . . the girl. . . ."

Hank wanted to stay with Casebolt, but he knew his partner was right. He got to his feet and hurried over to Victoria Knight. Somehow, Hank wasn't surprised as he recognized her. He started to drop to a knee beside her, but before he could, she surged up off the ground and threw herself into his arms, clutching desperately at him.

"I'm s-sorry," she gasped between hiccupping sobs.

"Are you hurt?" Hank asked her, aware that his voice was hard and cold.

Jerkily, Victoria shook her head and pressed her face against his chest.

"You let Parrish out, didn't you?" Hank demanded. "You gave him a gun." The words were an accusation, not a question.

After a long moment, Victoria nodded.

Hank took a deep breath, put his hands on her shoulders, gently moved her away from him. Anger blazed fiercely inside him, but taking it out on her wouldn't do any good now.

He turned away, ignoring the crying that still shook her. She needed her parents now, not him.

But he needed Sam Knight as well, he realized. The sheriff would have to put aside his search for his owlhoot brother for the time being and organize a posse to go after Brian Parrish.

Because Parrish was going to be brought back, Hank vowed grimly. Brought back and hung.

He knelt beside Casebolt and glanced at Buchanan long enough to snap, "Go find Sheriff Knight and anybody else you can hunt up. And get the doctor over here pronto!"

"S-sure, Ranger." The deputy stood up and hurried away.

Hank carefully lifted Casebolt's head and supported it on his leg. Casebolt's lips pulled back in a humorless grin. "Sawbones ain't goin' to help, son," he said. "I been shot . . . a heap of times before. . . . This'un's too bad. . . ."

"Dammit, don't talk like that, Joe!" Hank told him. "You're too tough for an outlaw's bullet to put down."

"Don't you . . . believe it." Casebolt somehow lifted a hand and clutched at Hank's sleeve. "You find Parrish, Hank. . . . You got to get Whitaker, too. . . . Get the job done, son, and wear that badge . . . proud. . . ." Casebolt took a deep shuddering breath, and for a second Hank thought he was gone, but then he said, as if surprised, "Well, by gum!"

"What is it, Joe?" Hank said.

"That bad tooth of mine . . . It don't hurt no more, Hank. . . . Don't hurt at all. . . ."

Chapter Eighteen

Sam Knight came running up a few minutes later, trailed by Buchanan. There were quite a few other townspeople following in the sheriff's wake, drawn by the gunfire and curious now that the shooting appeared to be over.

Hank saw Knight, but he would have walked right past him if the sheriff had not reached out and grabbed his arm. "How's Casebolt, Hank?" Knight asked tautly, looking past the Ranger at the figure on the ground.

"Dead," Hank said.

He jerked out of Knight's grip and started walking again.

The sheriff hurried after Hank. "Wait up, son," he said.

"The longer I wait the bigger start Parrish has," Hank replied coldly. "I need a fresh horse, Sheriff. Mine's played out after that ride today."

"That's fine. All the posse will have fresh mounts. But just hold on until we get organized."

Without pausing, Hank said, "You can get organized and then come after me. But I'm leaving now."

"Dammit." Knight grasped Hank's shoulder and hauled him to a stop. "Just slow down, Hank. You're going off half-cocked here."

Hank had to exert all his willpower to keep from lashing out at the sheriff. If Knight hadn't been so wrapped up in trying to catch his brother, Parrish might not have escaped.

That wasn't fair, Hank told himself as he took a deep breath. Knight couldn't be blamed for the actions of his daughter. Victoria was the one who had let Parrish loose to kill Casebolt.

Knight probably didn't know about that yet. Hank said, "You'd better go home and see to your daughter first, Sheriff. She's not hurt, but she's mighty upset."

"Victoria? What's she got to do with this?"

"Parrish has been courting her for a couple of weeks now. She's the one who helped him escape."

Knight stared at him, disbelief etched on his face.

This was partially his own fault, Hank realized. If he had told Knight that Victoria was showing an interest in Parrish, Knight would have stepped in and put a stop to it right away. Hank had wanted to give her the benefit of the doubt, though, had wanted her to realize for herself what a fool she was being. She had finally understood that, all right. It had come too late for Casebolt, though.

Hank started to turn away. "You follow me when you can, Sheriff. I'm heading out tonight."

"Can you track in the dark, Hank?" Knight's sharp voice stopped him.

Hank sighed. "Don't reckon I can."

"Well, neither can I. Neither can anybody else around here, as far as I know. But we can damn sure read sign in the morning when the sun comes up. If we start out before then, we're just wasting our time and maybe giving Parrish an even better chance to get away."

Hank sighed, then nodded. What Knight was saying made sense. "All right," he finally said. "We'll wait until morning. But I want to ride at first light."

"We'll be ready," Knight promised grimly. "Now I'm going home and see about what you told me. I reckon Victoria's there now?"

"She ran off headed in that direction," Hank told him. "From the looks of things, she's damned lucky Parrish didn't take her with him as a hostage."

"This whole thing's crazy, Hank. I just can't believe—" Knight shook his head. "I don't know what to believe. But I'm sorry as hell about Casebolt. Joe was a good man."

"He was," Hank agreed. "And I'm going to kill Brian Parrish."

Hank turned and walked away, heading for the hotel now. He tried to tell himself that this was better, that he could ride his own horse after the animal had had a night's rest. Knight was right about following the trail, too. It would be next to impossible to track Parrish in darkness.

But dawn was going to be a long time coming.

Hank was right. The rest of the night seemed a year long. He went back to the hotel and flung himself on his bed, but his eyes didn't close until about an hour before sunup. He kept staring at the ceiling and see-ing images of Joe Casebolt. His mind's eye saw the man laughing and drinking and fighting and grousing about his tooth.

Hank had only known Casebolt for a few months, but God, he was going to miss him.

And Parrish was going to pay for his death.

As Hank finally dozed off, though, he remembered what Casebolt had told him there in his last moments, fighting gallantly for the strength to express himself. Wear the badge proud, Casebolt had said. That meant upholding the law, just as they were sworn to. It meant bringing Parrish in alive if possible, to let the courts deal with him. That was a bitter pill, but Hank was going to swallow it.

He slept only a half-hour or so after that, then rolled stiffly off the bed and went downstairs and out in the bleak pre-dawn to saddle his horse. When he rode up in front of the sheriff's office a few minutes later, he found Knight waiting for him, along with more than a dozen other men. Hank saw Colonel Duffy, George Hay, Amasa Clark, Buck Hamilton, Jim Teague, and several other citizens he recognized. All of them were armed, and they all looked determined.

"We're ready, Hank," Knight said.

Hank nodded. "Let's ride."

The sun was beginning to creep above the horizon as the posse left Bandera, heading south away from the jail. Hank and Knight could see the tracks that Parrish's horse had made in the dusty trail. There had

155

been no rain and little wind since the night before, leaving the tracks in good shape.

"I did some asking around," Knight said to Hank as the two of them rode at the head of the posse. "That was one of old man Wynorski's horses that Parrish stole. Wynorski claims it's got plenty of sand and'll run all day without stopping."

Hank nodded. "Doesn't matter. We'll find him."

"I think you're right. Whitaker was always careful to hide his tracks. Looks like this boy was in such a hurry that he never thought of it."

Before they had gone a quarter of a mile, the trail swung west. The posse followed the tracks, and then a little farther on, Parrish had headed north again, swinging wide around Bandera.

"Looks to me like that fella is headed someplace in particular," Knight commented. "He charged out of town going hellbent-for-leather, not paying any attention to where he was going, but he started circling around soon enough."

Hank nodded. "Could be that Whitaker's got some sort of hide-out and that Parrish is heading for it."

"Some place we overlooked all those times we were searching for that outfit?"

"Could be," Hank shrugged. "There's not enough men or time to cover every square foot of this territory."

"True enough," Knight nodded. "If we were to get lucky, Whitaker and the rest of the gang might still be there. They've been lying low *somewhere* for a spell."

"Ever since your brother showed up." Hank kept his voice pitched low, so that the men riding behind them wouldn't hear.

"I'm . . . sorry about that, Hank. I know I've been neglecting things in town while I looked for Russ. I just sort of feel responsible for him. I know it doesn't make sense, but . . ."

"He *is* your brother. I reckon I can understand why you'd feel like you've got to track him down."

"There's always a chance I might be able to take him alive," Knight said. "Somebody else might not even try. They'd probably shoot first and worry about it later. Can't say as I'd blame them, either."

What the sheriff said made sense. Hank knew logically that there wasn't much Knight could have done to prevent Parrish's escape and

156

Casebolt's death. It had been pure bad luck, helped along by a love-struck girl. This morning, Hank couldn't even feel much anger toward Victoria Knight.

"How was your daughter this morning?" he asked Knight, surprising the sheriff with the note of concern in his voice.

"She was asleep when I left. The doc had to come by and give her something last night to help her sleep, she was so upset." Knight sighed heavily. "She admitted to me that she helped Parrish escape. As soon as we've got that boy back behind bars where he belongs, I'll talk to the county prosecutor about bringing charges against Victoria."

Hank shot a glance at him. "Your own daughter?"

"She helped a prisoner escape from jail," Knight said stonily. "That's a crime, Hank. You know that."

"Reckon I do," Hank replied quietly. He could see the strain that Knight was under, how the man was being torn in half by his devotion to the law and his love for his child.

Sam Knight had had bad luck all the way around, Hank thought. First his brother had gone bad, and now his daughter was in trouble. For a man like Knight, that had to be pure hell.

Around mid-morning, Knight reined in his horse, studied the tracks they had been following, and lifted his eyes to gaze at the horizon to the north. He said, "Parrish is heading for the pass. I'd stake my life on it."

While the trail had continued to lead them in a generally northward direction, there had been quite a few jogs and turns as Parrish followed gullies that became impassible with brush and deer trails that petered out. He hadn't been in the hill country for very long, Hank knew, and it looked like he was having trouble finding his way.

"You think Whitaker's hide-out is north of the pass?" Hank asked the sheriff.

"Could well be," Knight answered. "We've lost him before when he was heading north, even though it was well west of here. The pass is the easiest way out of the Medina Valley, but it's not the only one. There're other trails. And we've concentrated our searches south of those hills. I say we head straight for the pass. Maybe we can get there ahead of Parrish, or at least cut down his lead some. We can pick up his trail on the other side if he does get there first."

Hank considered for a long moment. He was inclined to believe that Knight was right.

"We'll give it a try," Hank said with a curt nod.

Knight put the spurs to his horse and sent it in a fast trot toward the distant pass. Hank fell in beside him, and the posse followed behind. They would take the most direct route now that they weren't trying to follow Parrish's tracks any more.

If they were wrong, Hank knew, there was a good chance that Parrish would be successful in slipping away from them. He would probably leave Bandera County far behind, maybe linking up with Whitaker again, maybe not.

But someday, Hank knew, he would face Parrish again. The blaze of hate he had felt for the outlaw had now cooled to embers that would never go out until Parrish had been brought to justice.

In grim silence, the posse rode through the bright morning sunshine toward Bandera Pass.

They reached the pass a little before noon. Hank had not tried to eat breakfast, knowing that his knotted-up stomach would not accept food when he got up that morning, but along the way he had gnawed on some jerky and cold biscuits George Hay had brought along. He had sipped some water from his canteen, too, but by all rights he still should have been hungry. He was too anxious to reach the head of the pass to worry about food, though.

The trail was too rocky for tracks to show, but once they made it to the top, there would be stretches where signs of Parrish's passage would be visible—provided the fleeing outlaw had already been here.

Hank noticed the way Sam Knight looked around as they rode through the pass. The sheriff's eyes were narrowed and there was a frown on his face. He was probably remembering the last time he had tracked an outlaw through this pass.

Knight reined in when they reached the top. He stared down at the ground, studying it. Hank was looking for sign, too, and he and Knight both spotted the tracks about the same time.

"Parrish has been here, all right," Knight said, gesturing toward the faint impressions in the dirt. "And not very long ago, I'd say. He's had to slow down some. Probably just about ran that stolen horse of Wynorski's into the ground last night."

"We can't be sure it was Parrish who made those tracks," Hank pointed out. "Could have been any pilgrim on his way through the pass."

"Not likely. Look at the length of that stride. The boy's still running that horse. He'll be lucky if it doesn't fall right out from under him, the way he's going."

Hank supposed the sheriff was right. The tracks probably had been made by Parrish. Having come to that decision, Hank heeled his horse forward, not wanting to waste any more time in talk.

There was a little grumbling from the posse, but Hank ignored it. He knew that he and Knight were pushing the men hard. It had to be done, though, if they were going to catch up to Parrish.

Once they were on the other side of the pass, the trail angled northwest. Hank had thought for a moment that Parrish was heading for Camp Verde again for some reason, but it soon became apparent he wasn't. The posse rode across a long, flat stretch, then entered another area of rugged, live-oak–covered hills. When Hank looked back over his shoulder, he could see the Twin Sisters far, far in the distance. Up ahead were more hills with deep, twisting, shadow-choked gullies between them. It was some of the most forbidding terrain Hank had encountered on this assignment.

It became more difficult to follow Brian Parrish's trail, but the signs they could see told them the outlaw wasn't far ahead now. Hank felt anticipation growing inside him. His hand strayed down to touch the stock of the Henry rifle that rode in his saddle boot.

He hoped Parrish would put up a fight.

The posse followed the tracks into one of the narrow canyons. The slopes pressed in close on both sides, and several of the men glanced around nervously. This would make a fine place for an ambush, and the posse members knew it. A little creek ran through the canyon, the stream only a few feet wide and shallow over a rocky bed, but the water ran fast and clear and cold. Every few yards, a hoofprint was visible in the softer ground next to the creek. Parrish had come this way, all right.

They followed the creek all the way to where it bubbled out of a stone wall.

The canyon was a dead end.

Hank stared at the rock. It was impossible. Parrish had come this way; Hank was sure of it. The walls were too steep for him to have left it since the last place they had seen his tracks.

Knight looked just as baffled. He sat on his horse and rubbed his jaw in thought. Finally, he said, "There's got to be another way out of here."

Hank nodded. "Parrish had to go somewhere, all right."

When Knight spoke again, his voice was soft, pitched so that it couldn't be heard more than a few feet away. "I'm not going to point to it," he said to Hank, "but do you see that clump of brush there to the right of the springs?"

Hank looked, but he followed the sheriff's lead and didn't nod. "I see it," he said, equally quietly.

"I'd be willing to bet that there's a trail behind it. Wouldn't have to be much, just wide enough to let a man on horseback through."

"Reckon there's a pocket back there where Whitaker and his men could hide?"

"That'd be my guess," Knight said. "They'd have good water close by, and nobody would come up into this hole without a damn good reason. Easy to guard, too."

"You think they've got a sentry posted?"

"You know Whitaker better'n I do. What do you think?"

Hank said grimly, "He'd have a guard, all right. What do we do now?"

"First thing is to make sure that's really where they're hiding out." Knight turned around in his saddle and raised his voice as he addressed the rest of the posse. "Sorry, boys, but it looks like we've lost him. Nothing we can do now but head back to Bandera."

There were relieved looks on the faces of most of the men. They turned their horses around and started back down the canyon. Hank and Knight were bringing up the rear now.

"Soon as we get around that bend, you and I will drop off our horses and head back on foot," Knight said. "There's plenty of cover, and if there is an owlhoot back there keeping an eye on the entrance, he'll think we've gone back with the rest of the posse."

"That's about all we can do," Hank agreed. The plan was risky, he knew, but he found himself looking forward to it. The chance not only to get Parrish but to capture Whitaker and the rest of the gang made the young Ranger's pulse race.

When the posse was out of sight of the canyon's end, Knight called a halt. The other men turned surprised faces toward the sheriff and listened intently as he explained the plan. "You boys hear shooting, you come a-running," Knight told them. "Head for the brush to the right of that spring."

The men nodded their agreement and started checking their guns. Hank and Knight swung down from their saddles and tied their mounts to a tree. Hank slid the Henry out of the saddle boot and put an extra handful of cartridges for it into his shirt pocket. Knight took a bullet from his shell belt and loaded the empty chamber of his Colt.

Then the two lawmen headed back the way they had come, veering over to the slope and using the thick trunks of the live oaks for cover.

Hank let Knight take the lead. The older man had more experience at this sort of thing. Sneaking back up the canyon like this made Hank feel like they were fighting Indians rather than outlaws. Even Comanches couldn't be any more savage than Isom Whitaker, Brian Parrish, and the other members of the gang, though.

Hank and Knight catfooted their way back to the head of the stream. There was a narrow ledge across the face of the rock wall above the spring. Climbing to it wasn't easy, but they managed. Hank's face was beaded with sweat by the time they reached the ledge and began edging across it.

Knight was still in the lead. When he reached the far end of the ledge, he reached back and stopped Hank without a word. The sheriff leaned forward. From this angle, he would be able to see behind that clump of brush, Hank thought.

A moment later, Knight straightened and glanced over at Hank. A grim nod told the story. Knight's suspicions had been correct. He motioned for Hank to take his place. The ledge was barely wide enough for them to change places, but they managed without either one of them falling into the spring a dozen feet below.

Hank followed Knight's example and leaned out to look behind the brush. There was a trail there, all right, with a dogleg entrance that was screened off by the brush and an outcropping of rock.

Across the narrow, steep-sided gully where the trail ran was another ledge, and sitting behind a boulder that perched there was a man with a rifle. Hank could see only a booted foot and the muzzle of a rifle, but that was enough.

Hank drew back and leaned against the rock face. "What now?" he asked Knight.

The sheriff jerked a thumb upward. "Think you can go up the side of this?"

Hank studied the rock. There were some rough places that might provide handholds and footholds, but it would be a tough climb. Still, if he could manage it, he would be able to get above the pocket that had to be hidden back in there.

"I'm not a blasted mountain goat, but I'm willing to give it a try," he said after a moment of thought. It would be worth the risk, he decided.

"I'd do it myself, but I'm not as young as I used to be," Knight said. "If you can get up there, I can pick off the guard from here if he starts taking potshots at you. We've got Whitaker and the others bottled up in there. You start 'em running this way, and they'll run right into me and the posse. We can take them, Hank."

"If they're up there," Hank pointed out.

"They're there," Knight said with a nod. "My gut tells me that. This is the showdown, Hank."

The sheriff was right. Hank said, "Give me your belt."

Knight frowned but complied with the request. Hank took the belt and quickly rigged a sling for the Henry rifle so that it could ride on his back while he was climbing.

When Hank was ready to go, Knight held out his hand. "Good luck, son," the sheriff said sincerely. "I'll be watching your back."

Hank shook hands with him. "Just be watching for Whitaker and the others when they come bolting out of there."

Then he turned to face the rock wall, reached up to get a handhold, began to climb.

Chapter Nineteen

Hank had told Knight the truth: He was no mountain goat. He had less than twenty feet of rock face to cover, but several times during the climb he had to dig in with his fingers and the toes of his boots and hang on for dear life until he felt he could go on.

Eventually, though, he reached the top of the slope and pulled himself over, sprawling on a rocky bench dotted with scrub brush. The bench ran back a couple of hundred yards to another hill. Hank lifted himself to his feet, being careful not to dislodge any rocks that might tumble into the narrow cleft and alert the guard.

All hell would be popping soon enough without getting an early start on it.

Hank unslung the rifle and took Knight's belt loose from it. He started forward, paralleling the hidden trail but not getting too close to it.

A moment later he spotted a thin haze of smoke in the air ahead of him. There was a camp up there, all right, and whoever had built the fire knew how to disguise it as much as was possible. Hank bellied down when he saw the little pocket valley opening up. He crawled forward until he could look down into the bowl in the earth.

There was no telling what freak of nature had carved out this place, but it made a hell of a hide-out for men on the dodge. As far as Hank could tell, there was only the one way in; the slopes surrounding the valley were too steep for horses to climb. A man might be able to make it up the sides, especially since there were quite a few small trees to hang on to. The valley was maybe a quarter of a mile long and only half that wide.

This was the true origin of the creek that the posse had followed, Hank saw. It came to the surface from underground springs at the far end of the valley, then disappeared again into the rock somewhere beneath him, only to emerge once more on the far side, where Knight was waiting. The stream ensured that there was plenty of grass for the horses that were grazing calmly in a rope corral. There were a dozen animals there.

Someone had found this hideaway valley before Isom Whitaker. There was a cabin down there, a ramshackle structure made of logs. There were several men standing around the front of the cabin. Hank recognized some of them from the shoot-out at Camp Verde. They were part of Whitaker's bunch, no doubt about that.

As Hank watched, his pulse pounding in his head, Isom Whitaker himself appeared in the doorway of the cabin. The outlaw leader was bareheaded at the moment, and his curly red hair was impossible to miss. Behind him came a lean, bearded figure carrying a bottle of whiskey. Hank's breath caught in his throat as he recognized Brian Parrish.

Any good memories he might have had of Parrish from their boyhood in San Saba were long gone. It was all Hank could do not to lift the Henry and put a slug in the bastard's head.

Instead he took a deep breath and forced himself to count the men he could see. There were seven in the clearing in front of the cabin, including Whitaker and Parrish. With the man on guard duty, that made eight. Four men were unaccounted for, but there was a good chance they were inside the cabin, sleeping or playing cards.

There was no point in waiting. Hank raised himself on his elbows and yelled, "Whitaker! This is the Texas Rangers! Surrender in the name of the law!"

Then he triggered a warning shot, the bullet slamming into the dirt at Isom Whitaker's feet.

Whitaker let out a howl and flung himself backward, grabbing for his holstered pistol as he did so. That was all Hank had time to see. He was rolling as fast as he could to a new position several feet away, at the same time levering another shell into the rifle's chamber. Without coming to a complete stop, he fired again, not really caring at this point where the slug went. Then he was moving again, stopping, shooting, rolling, stopping, shooting . . .

It wouldn't fool them for long, but the gang might think there was a whole company of Rangers up here surrounding them. That thought might spook them into making a run for it.

The sudden crackle of gunfire down the trail added to the illusion of a large-scale attack. Hank knew that was Knight taking care of the guard, but Whitaker and the others wouldn't know that.

Whitaker shouted, "Kill the sons-of-bitches!"

Some of the men followed orders and started snapping shots at the rim, making Hank duck back. But the others were already running for their horses and throwing saddles onto the animals. Hank saw through the powdersmoke that his hunch about the other men had been correct. Four of them came boiling out of the cabin and joined in the general panic.

He saw Parrish crouching behind a bush and firing at him with a revolver. Probably the same gun he had used to kill Casebolt, Hank thought. He slapped the Henry to his shoulder and squeezed the trigger. The bullet screamed close by Parrish's ear and made him dive for better cover.

All the outlaws except Parrish and Whitaker were making for the cleft where the trail was. Whitaker screamed for them to come back, but no one was paying any attention to him. Hank's ruse had worked. They had been thrown into momentary panic.

Seeing their flight, Hank rolled back away from the edge of the bench and surged to his feet, then ran toward the rock wall he had climbed to reach this position. The posse would have heard the shooting by now and would be charging back down the canyon. When they ran head-on into the fleeing outlaws, the odds would be pretty even.

Hank and Knight might be able to swing those odds.

Hank reached the spot where he had climbed onto the bench just as the first of the bandits emerged from the hidden trail. The man hauled his mount around the sharp turn and burst through the screen of brush. Hank held his fire and glanced down at the ledge where he had left Knight. The sheriff was still crouched there. He looked up and waved his Colt at Hank. There was a broad grin on Knight's face, the first smile Hank had seen there in days.

Hank didn't feel like smiling. Not yet.

The posse rounded the bend, guns in hand, as the other outlaws poured out into the canyon. The narrow confines of the place erupted in gunfire as both groups tried to pull their mounts to a stop. Several of the horses stumbled and fell, and in places the fight was suddenly hand to hand.

Hank and Knight opened fire from their position behind the outlaws, catching them in a crossfire. Hank's shots knocked a couple of Whitaker's men out of their saddles, and the sheriff downed two more before he had to stop to reload. In the meantime, the deputized citizens of Bandera were giving a good account of themselves. Hank blinked his eyes against the sting of powdersmoke and tried to spot Whitaker and Parrish.

As he lowered his rifle, the gunfire stopped abruptly. In the sudden silence the only sound was the whimpering of a wounded man. Six wounded outlaws were sprawled bloodily on the ground, and only one of them was moving. The three who were unhurt had dropped their guns and lifted their hands in surrender.

Whitaker and Parrish were nowhere to be seen, Hank realized.

In the eerie lull, the sound of hoofbeats came to his ears.

Hank twisted around. The knowledge that he had been wrong lanced into him like a white-hot knife. A man *could* get horses up out of that pocket valley, if he was desperate enough.

And Whitaker and Parrish were certainly desperate.

Hank flung the rifle to his shoulder as he saw the two riders cresting the hill on the far side of the hide-out. He fired as fast as he could work the lever, emptying the rest of the shells in the Henry's magazine. But even as he sent lead flying after them, he knew it was too late.

They were gone.

"What is it, Hank?" he heard Sam Knight calling from below him.

With a deep sense of failure, Hank lowered the rifle from his shoulder. He stared at the spot where the two outlaws had disappeared, then turned and said in a bleak voice, "Whitaker and Parrish got away."

Knight cursed. "Which way are they headed?"

"East."

"Reckon you might as well come on down from there. They don't have too big a lead on us just yet."

That was true, Hank thought. He bent over and picked up the belt he had dropped earlier and reslung the rifle on his back. The climb down didn't take as long as the one going up, because when he was within four or five feet of the ledge, he let go and dropped the rest of the way. Knight was waiting to grab his arm and steady him when he landed.

Hank looked down the canyon and saw that the other members of the posse had things well under control. George Hay and some of the others had tied up the outlaws who had surrendered, leaving them on horseback and binding their hands behind them. The stray horses had been rounded up and their dead masters lashed onto their backs. One horse carried a double burden, as a couple of the men from Bandera had climbed to the ledge overlooking the hidden trail and retrieved the body of the guard that Knight had shot. None of the posse members had been killed in the fighting, and as far as Hank could tell, there were no serious injuries, only a few scrapes and bruises and bullet creases.

The two lawmen climbed down off the ledge and reclaimed their mounts from the posse. As Knight swung up into the saddle, he said to Hay, "George, you reckon you and the other fellas can get these prisoners back to Bandera all right?"

"Sure can, Sheriff," the shopkeeper and temporary deputy answered. "All the fight's been knocked out of 'em. The ones that are still alive, that is."

"Ranger Littleton and I are going after the ones that got away, then," Knight declared. He glanced at Hank. "That all right with you?"

Hank nodded wordlessly. If Knight hadn't offered to go along, he would have ridden after Whitaker and Parrish by himself.

"I know a few shortcuts that Whitaker might not," Knight went on. "We'll circle around, see if we can pick up their trail and figure out where they're headed."

Hank urged his horse forward and fell in beside the sheriff. Knight waved farewell to his men. Hank didn't look back at the place where the gunfight had taken place. He had put that out of his mind. Whitaker's gang was destroyed, but the outlaw leader was still on the loose. The job wouldn't be finished until Whitaker himself was dead or a prisoner. Hank intended to finish that job—for Joe Casebolt.

"You may have been smart starting out, but you've turned into a goddamn idiot!" Whitaker snapped at Brian Parrish.

The two men had slowed their horses to a trot, trying to save some of the animals' strength in case they had to make another dash for freedom later. Parrish cut his eyes over at Whitaker and said, "I don't have to take that kind of shit off you, Isom. You're a fine one to talk, after the way you left me to rot in that jail for weeks!"

"I would've busted you out before you got sent to prison," Whitaker growled. "You told me yourself those Rangers were watching the place. What did you want, Parrish, for all of us to ride into a trap?"

"Like we did at Camp Verde?" Parrish blazed back. His hand strayed to the butt of one of the Remingtons tucked behind his belt.

"I wouldn't," Whitaker said flatly. "I'm mad enough at you, boy, the way you led that posse right to the hide-out. I wouldn't mind shooting you myself right about now."

Parrish grimaced and took his hand away from the gun. He knew damn well that Whitaker meant it. After a few moments of silence, he said, "So what do we do now?"

Whitaker looked around. They had left the hidden valley in such a hurry that he had lost his bearings to a certain extent. They were somewhere northwest of Bandera Pass, but that was about all he knew at the moment. And these craggy hills all looked alike.

"They'll be coming after us," he finally said. "I reckon the best thing to do would be for us to split up."

Parrish shook his head. "I don't much like that idea."

"I don't care whether you like it or not," Whitaker replied. "That's what we're going to do, at least until we see if we've thrown them off. You remember that sinkhole on Verde Creek?"

"About two miles west of the store and the old camp? I remember."

"We'll meet up there, late this afternoon," Whitaker decided. "If it's all clear, we'll hit the store for some traveling money, then head north. I want to leave this part of the country behind me."

"It was good to us for a while," Parrish mused.

"Until Russ Knight showed up." Whitaker snorted. "He got the countryside even more stirred up than we did."

Parrish frowned. "Knight? You talking about the sheriff?"

"His brother. Reckon you didn't hear about it, stuck in jail like you were."

"There were a lot of things I didn't hear about, I reckon," Parrish said sharply, his resentment coming to the surface again.

"The sheriff's got a brother who's as big an outlaw as you and me, kid. Russ Knight works alone, though. Foolhardy, if you ask me. But he pulled some good jobs the last couple of weeks."

"Maybe they'll forget about us and worry about him instead."

Whitaker shook his head. "Not if you killed that old Ranger, they won't. Littleton won't, anyway. He'll just keep coming . . . until somebody kills him."

"Sounds like a good idea to me," Parrish said with a savage grin.

Whitaker reined in his horse as they entered a grove of trees. "We'll split up here. Remember, that sinkhole, late this afternoon."

"I'll be there," Parrish promised.

"Don't bring the law with you this time," Whitaker snapped. Then he put the spurs to his horse and galloped away, still going east. Parrish watched him for a moment, then headed off, bearing north. That would mean some backtracking to Verde Creek later in the day, but it would be worth the extra miles if he could shake off Hank Littleton.

An hour later, Sam Knight reined in as he passed the same grove of trees and pointed. "Look there," he said to Hank. "Almost missed them."

Hank swung down from the saddle and knelt beside the tracks, studying them in the shade of an elm. "They split up," he said.

"Reckon we'd best do the same."

Hank stared at the tracks. "I wonder which one is Whitaker and which one is Parrish."

"Does it matter?"

Hank looked up at the sheriff for a moment, then shook his head. "I don't suppose it does. I want them both."

Whitaker indicated the trail that led east through the trees. "I'll take this fella. You can have the one that veered off north. That all right with you?''

Hank nodded. He got back on his horse and turned the animal's head north.

Isom Whitaker had spent some of the time since he had parted company with Parrish wondering if he should bother to show up on Verde Creek or not. It would be simple enough to abandon the young fool, he thought. Parrish had been a good right-hand man for a long time, but everybody wore out his usefulness sooner or later. Maybe the time had come to cut and run, and be damned to everybody else.

Whitaker gave a shake of his head. He couldn't do that to Parrish, even if the boy's brain had been muddled by his stay in Bandera's jail.

Whitaker found a game trail that led him around a particularly rough stretch of hills, and then the terrain flattened out somewhat. He was entering the valley of Verde Creek, he knew. He was closer to the rendezvous point and would reach it first. That was all right. It would give him a chance to find a hiding place and make sure no one was following Parrish when he arrived.

As he rode past a little draw that had been cut by the run-off of some of the hill country's heavy rainstorms, he heard the sharp click of a horseshoe on stone. Whitaker's instincts sent his hand flashing toward the gun on his hip, but before he could reach it, a cold voice rapped, "Don't!"

Whitaker froze. His hand was still several inches from the butt of his gun, and he knew from the tone of the other man's voice that he would never complete the draw successfully. Whoever had gotten the drop on him would have his gun out and ready and could blow Whitaker out of the saddle in an instant.

A man rode out of the draw and circled around Whitaker, and sure enough, there was a big Colt clutched in his fist. The stranger carried himself like he knew how to use it and wouldn't hesitate for a second to do so. There was a broad grin on his face as he regarded Whitaker.

The outlaw leader glared at him. "Well, mister, you're calling the tune. What's it going to be?"

"Don't know me, do you, Whitaker?" the man asked. He was big and competent looking.

Whitaker shook his head. "Can't say as I do. Should I?"

The man reached into his shirt pocket and said, "I reckon you could figure out who I am, happen I was wearing *this*." He held up a shiny metal star that bounced sunlight off its polished surface.

"Sheriff Knight," Whitaker said emotionlessly, making the logical guess.

"Well, you're half right," the man chuckled. Suddenly, he flung the badge away from him. It went spinning up into the air, and the gun in his hand blasted. Whitaker flinched involuntarily, but the man had altered his aim. The slug hit the badge, punching a hole through it and knocking it crazily to one side. The ruined symbol landed in the dust of the trail. The man had his gun leveled at Whitaker again before the stunned outlaw could move.

"What the hell . . . ?" Whitaker gasped.

Abruptly, the man he had taken to be Sheriff Sam Knight holstered his pistol. "Reckon it's about time for the good sheriff to retire," he said. "Sam Knight's dead, Whitaker. My brother's been dead ever since I killed him in Bandera Pass over a year ago. Now, considering that we're both too smart for the Rangers and the rest of the folks around here, what say you and I team up for a while?"

Whitaker kept staring at Russ Knight for a long moment, then he threw back his head and began to laugh. He laughed for a long time.

Chapter Twenty

As he rode after the fugitive—whichever one it was—Hank thought back on the job that had brought him to the hill country. It had been less than a month since he and Casebolt had been given the assignment in Captain McNelly's Austin office, but it seemed a lot longer than that.

Maybe it would end today. Hank fervently hoped so. He wasn't sure at this point if he wanted to continue in the Ranger service or not, but he would at least finish this assignment.

Tracking had never been his greatest talent, but he had learned a few things from his father and Casebolt and Buffalo Newcomb and he was managing to follow the tracks left by the man he was chasing. From time to time, he lost the trail, but he always picked it up again fairly quickly.

In the late afternoon, the tracks turned east, then south again after a mile or so. The outlaw was doubling back for some reason.

Hank hoped the man he was after was Brian Parrish. Whitaker had to be caught, of course, but he had a personal score to settle with Parrish.

He rode down out of the hills and into a broad, flat valley. A few minutes later, Hank spotted a line of green up ahead that marked a creek. And about halfway between him and that creek was a lone rider. Hank's breath caught in his throat. The man was over half a mile away, but even at that distance, Hank could tell that there was something familiar about him.

Hank put the spurs to his horse, urging more speed out of the animal's tired frame.

Something must have warned the man up ahead, because he swiveled in the saddle and gazed back the way he had come. Hank could see the beard on the man's face now, confirming his identity. It was Parrish, all right. The way the man suddenly leaned forward and put his own horse into a desperate gallop was the last bit of evidence Hank needed.

The range was too great even for a rifle. Hank had to cut down the gap between them. He leaned over his horse's neck, patting the animal and uttering words of encouragement that were whipped away by the wind.

Hank glanced from side to side and studied the landmarks. This valley looked familiar, and he realized suddenly that the stream ahead of him was Verde Creek. From the looks of the hills, the store where Parrish had originally been captured was probably several miles east.

Hank saw puffs of smoke coming from Parrish's hand as the outlaw twisted in the saddle again. Parrish was firing at him with a handgun. A grim smile creased Hank's face. At this range Parrish was just wasting bullets.

Hank slid the Henry out of the saddle boot. The creek was lined with huge cypresses. If Parrish reached them, their trunks would provide him with plenty of cover. Hank wanted to stop him before he got there. He tried one shot from horseback, saw the slug kick up dust a good twenty yards behind Parrish's lunging horse. Still too far away, Hank thought. He tried to get more speed out of the gallant mount underneath him.

He wasn't going to make it. Hank could see that now. Parrish was only a hundred yards from the creek. He would reach the trees within moments.

Resolve hardened within Hank. He had come this far. He was not going to let Parrish get away again. Even if it meant charging right into the bastard's guns.

He saw Parrish reining in as he reached the trees along the creek

173

bank. Parrish threw himself off the horse and behind a massive cypress. The outlaw thrust one of his pistols around the trunk and started firing.

Hank crouched in the saddle, guiding the horse with his knees now, using all the horsemanship at his command. He veered to one side as he jacked another cartridge into the Henry, then brought the rifle to his shoulder and pressed the trigger. The bullet thumped into the trunk of the tree that Parrish was using for cover, making him duck back.

Hank left the saddle, flinging himself to the right as his horse headed left. He landed on his feet, ran forward a few steps, and then his momentum took him down. He rolled, came up about fifty feet from the creek bank, the rifle still in his hands.

Parrish loosed a shot at the galloping horse, instinct making him pull the trigger even though he could see that the saddle was now empty. Hank ran toward him, firing twice more from the hip. Parrish jerked back, suddenly losing his footing as some of the creek bank crumbled beneath him. He rolled a couple of feet, then caught himself against a big root that extended from another tree and came up on one knee.

Hank skidded to a halt ten feet away, leveling the rifle at Parrish. The outlaw brought his pistol up, earing back the hammer. Both men froze, staring at each other over the barrels of their guns.

"Drop it, Parrish," Hank said. "I'll kill you if you don't."

Parrish's voice was breathless from his fall as he replied, "Or I'll kill you, Hank. Sorry it had to come to this, pard. We had some good times, a long ways back."

"Sorry won't bring Joe Casebolt back," Hank grated.

Parrish's face suddenly twisted. "Then kill me and get it over with, goddamn it! Or I'll kill you! Why don't we both just die right here and now, Hank? Get it over with!"

Hank saw Parrish's finger whiten on the trigger. He threw himself forward as the gun in the outlaw's hand blasted. The bullet whined past Hank's head as he lashed out with the rifle. The barrel of the Henry cracked across Parrish's wrist, knocking the pistol away. Hank landed on his knees and brought the stock of the rifle around as Parrish grabbed desperately for the other gun stuck behind his belt. The butt of the Henry smacked into his jaw before he could reach it, knocking him sprawling on the bank.

Hank grabbed the outlaw's second gun and jerked it free, then sprang back to cover him with the rifle. He drew a deep, ragged breath, then said, "It's over, Parrish."

Parrish pushed himself up on an elbow, let out a moan as he rubbed his swelling jaw, and glared at Hank with cold hatred.

"Get on your feet," Hank told him. "You're going to catch our horses, and then we're going back to Bandera."

"Why didn't you just go ahead and shoot me?" Parrish asked thickly.

Hank took his left hand off the rifle long enough to reach up and tap the silver star on a silver circle that was pinned to his shirt. "I'm a law-man," he said, and meant it.

His doubts were gone. Maybe this assignment hadn't gone well, but he had done his best. That was all any man could do. Joe Casebolt sure as hell hadn't been a quitter, and Hank knew now that he couldn't be, either. He was a Ranger for as long as they wanted him.

"Come on," he said to Parrish. "We've got a long way to go yet, and it'll be getting dark before too long."

He wondered how Sam Knight had fared with his pursuit of Whitaker.

Forty yards away, behind a clump of brush, Russ Knight reached out and grasped Isom Whitaker's arm, forcing down the hand that held a gun. "Not here," Russ said quietly.

"Why not?" Whitaker snapped. "We can kill that Ranger and set Brian free, then get the hell out of this part of the country."

A reckless smile tugged at Russ Knight's mouth. "I've got a better idea," he said. "Something more fitting. I told you I was going to call the shots if we rode together, Whitaker."

"I know," the outlaw said grudgingly. "That doesn't mean I have to like it. Reckon you know what you're doing, though, the way you've fooled everybody."

"That's right." Russ turned his horse. "Now come on. It'll take Littleton and Parrish a few minutes to get mounted up and back on the trail. We can reach the pass ahead of them without any trouble."

Slowly, Whitaker returned Russ's smile. "Bandera Pass, eh? I guess that would be more fitting. That's where you turned the tables on every-body else before."

At first Whitaker had been reluctant to believe that Russ Knight could have taken his brother's place and played the part so convincingly as to fool the people of Bandera, including the sheriff's family. But when he thought back over what had happened during the last couple of weeks, he had to admit that it explained how Russ had been able to pull so many robberies without ever coming close to being caught. All it had taken was some circling around and a few changes of clothes to convince everyone else in the county that Sheriff Sam Knight was always in the wrong place at the wrong time. Whitaker had sent his men out from the hidden valley from time to time to buy supplies, and they brought back stories of how Russ Knight was running rings around the law in Bandera County.

You couldn't help but admire the man, for both his ruthlessness and his cunning.

They had reached the meeting place on Verde Creek before Parrish got there. When they spotted him coming, Whitaker had wanted to ride out to meet him, but Russ had noticed someone on Parrish's trail. They had pulled back into the brush to wait and see what was going on and had witnessed the shoot-out between Hank and Parrish. It had all happened too quickly for them to be much help to Parrish, and Russ had stopped Whitaker when he did try to step in.

It galled Whitaker to take orders after so many years of giving them, but he had seen something in Russ's eyes that made him play along. Those eyes burned with an intensity that told him there was a good chance Russ Knight was a little bit crazy. Maybe more than a little bit . . .

But ambushing Hank Littleton in Bandera Pass—Whitaker had to admit that that was a damned good idea.

That self-righteous son-of-a-bitch Ranger was finally going to get what was coming to him.

And he could always kill Russ Knight later, Whitaker decided.

The sun was drooping close to the western slope of the pass as Hank and Parrish rode into it. It cast shadows over the trail and left a garish red glow in the air. A hot, dry wind came up out of the south and blew in the faces of the two riders.

Parrish was in the lead. Hank had tied his hands to the saddlehorn and kept the Henry trained on his prisoner's back. Parrish wasn't going to get away again.

There had been little said between the two men since leaving Verde Creek. There was still a long ride back to Bandera, and it would be well after dark before they got there. Hank thought that the posse should have been back in town for quite a while now. The jail would be crowded, and the undertaker would have plenty of work to do.

He had hoped to run into Sam Knight before now. Whitaker was the only loose end left. If Knight could manage to corral him, that would finally bring to a close the job that had led Hank and Casebolt to Bandera.

Idly, Hank wondered what would happen to Victoria Knight. He couldn't imagine a jury sending her to prison, even if she was convicted. It was even possible that the county prosecutor wouldn't want to bring charges against her. If that happened, Hank supposed he would have to live with the decision, even if she was partially to blame for Casebolt's death.

Parrish was the one who had pulled the trigger, though. And he would hang for it. Hank didn't doubt that for a second.

The shot slammed out in the early evening stillness, and Hank blinked as something zipped past his ear. A second blast came hard on the heels of the first. A slug plucked at the sleeve of Hank's shirt.

Instinct took over. He let out a yell and kicked his horse into a gallop. As he caught up to Parrish's horse, he smacked the animal across the rump with the Henry, starting it running. Parrish shouted, "What the hell . . . !"

Out of the corner of his eye, Hank saw the muzzle flashes coming from both slopes of the pass. One of the bushwhackers had to be Whitaker, but who was the other one? No time to worry about that, he thought. He brought the rifle to his shoulder and started to fire as he and Parrish dashed down the rocky trail.

Bullets sang around his head. It was like running a gauntlet, a gauntlet that led straight down through Bandera Pass. If they could reach the bottom, he might have a chance to get away with his prisoner.

A slug thudded into the chest of Parrish's horse, and suddenly the animal was falling. Parrish was flung out of the saddle, but his hands tied to the saddlehorn kept him from being thrown clear. He screamed in agony as the horse landed on him and rolled over his legs, snapping one and crushing the other.

Hank jerked his horse to the side as Parrish and his mount went down in front of him, desperately trying to miss them. But then his own horse stumbled and started to fall. Hank kicked his feet out of the stirrups and tightened his grip on the rifle as he left the saddle. He hit hard, the rocky trail slamming into his shoulder. Somehow he managed to hang on to the Henry.

A rider burst out of the trees on the eastern slope of the pass. Hank heard the beat of hooves and looked up, shaking his head to clear his vision. He saw Isom Whitaker galloping toward him. There was a revolver in the outlaw's hand, and flame and noise belched from its muzzle.

Hank rolled to the side as slugs punched into the trail where he had been an instant earlier. He came up onto his feet, calling on all the cool nerve he possessed. Instinct and years of practice socked the butt of the Henry into his shoulder as another bullet whined past him. His cheek rested on the smooth wood of the stock, and both eyes were open as he lined the blade of the sight on Whitaker's shirt pocket.

Hank fired, and the outlaw was flung backward like he had run into a stone wall. Whitaker flopped lifelessly on the hard ground as his horse raced on, riderless now.

For a long moment, Hank stayed where he was. Then he took a deep breath and started to turn around to check on Parrish.

His legs went out from under him. He fell heavily, his strength deserting him. The Henry slipped out of his hands and clattered down the trail a few feet.

Hank pushed himself up on an elbow and looked down at himself. There was a large red stain on his shirt, low down on the right side. He stared at it for a long moment. One of the bullets had hit him after all. During the heat of the battle, he hadn't even noticed.

As best he could tell, the slug had just torn through some of the meat of his right side, missing anything important. Quite a bit of blood had leaked out of the wound, though, and that was where the danger would lie.

Hank blinked at the sound of footsteps, turned his head to look over his shoulder. The second bushwhacker! He had been concentrating on Isom Whitaker and had forgotten about the other man. Now, Hank saw him coming out of the brush on the west side of the pass, his figure emerging from the shadows.

There was a gun in the man's hand. Hank glanced around and saw the Henry lying on the rocks a few feet away. He lifted himself, gathering his strength to lunge toward the fallen rifle.

A bullet spanged off the trail between him and the Henry. A familiar voice warned, "Don't even try it, Littleton."

Hank turned, shock etched on his face.

The man striding purposefully toward him was Sheriff Sam Knight.

"Sheriff!" Hank cried. "What—"

Then he saw that Knight wasn't wearing his badge. Not only that, there was an arrogant grin on the man's face unlike any expression Hank had ever seen on Sam Knight.

The realization that he was facing Russ Knight, not Sam, sank in on Hank's stunned brain. And yet this man was wearing the same clothes as the sheriff had been. . . .

"Trying to figure it out, aren't you?" the man said as he came to a stop a few feet from Hank. "You and that stupid partner of yours never stopped to wonder why Sam couldn't seem to catch me, did you? You never thought that Sam Knight, the sheriff, and Russ Knight, the outlaw, might be *the same man*!"

The wound in Hank's side was starting to hurt now. He looked up at Knight, not moving. There was nothing he could do. His Colt was still in its holster, but he wasn't a fast draw even under the best of circumstances.

"Fooled you, just like I fooled everybody else," Knight boasted. He lifted the gun in his hand slightly, centering the barrel on Hank's forehead. "Reckon it's time for you to die, Ranger."

"No," Hank said.

Knight paused, frowning at him.

Even in this desperate situation, questions were racing through Hank's head. And there was a single answer to all of them, hideous though it was.

"No," he said again. "Russ Knight never could've fooled Sam's wife and daughter. Faye and Victoria would have known the difference if Russ had come back from here a year ago. You may *think* you're Russ Knight, mister, but you're not."

"Dammit, I know who I am," the man snarled. "Haven't I been pulling off holdups all over the county for two weeks?"

"Still doesn't make you Russ Knight." Hank knew he was stalling, but at the same time, he hoped he could break through to the real identity of the man holding a gun on him. He didn't think that Sam Knight would shoot him.

If he was right about his guess—and if there was anything of Sam Knight left inside the killer looming above him.

"What about Susie?" Knight demanded. "She was sure as hell convinced I'm Russ Knight. Hell, you should have heard her moaning and carrying on when I bedded her."

Hank felt a ball of sickness rolling around inside his belly. He didn't know if it was from his injury or what he was hearing . . . or both. He swallowed and said, "Susie Brewer hadn't seen Russ Knight in a year herself. Memories can get fuzzy in that time, Sam. But Faye and Victoria saw you every day, all along, before and after that gunfight here."

The muzzle of Knight's revolver started to tremble slightly. "Don't call me that name!" he grated. He raised his free hand and wiped it over a face that had gone deathly pale. "I'm Russ Knight, goddamn it. Russ . . ."

His eyes closed for a moment, and his head drooped. Hank could have made a play then, but he held his breath and waited instead. Any sudden move might ruin everything.

Seconds passed like hours, and then Sam Knight opened his eyes and looked up. Hank had never seen more pain in a man's gaze. He turned the gun in his hand, raised it to stare at it in horror. Slowly, he said, "I kept having those dreams . . . like Russ was haunting me. They always stopped just as I . . . I shot him down."

"You had to kill him, Sheriff," Hank said quietly. "He was trying to kill you. He was an outlaw, and you were just doing your job."

"But he was still my brother!" The words ripped hoarsely out of Knight's throat. He took several deep, shuddering breaths, then looked up at the crest of the eastern slope. "I buried him up there. Then I went back to Bandera and told everybody he had gotten away. Seemed the shame in letting Russ escape was less than the hurt of admitting I'd killed him."

"I'm sorry, Sheriff. I really am."

Knight nodded, but he didn't seem to really see Hank now as he glanced back at him. "Those dreams just kept coming back. I couldn't ever get away from them. And then that Brewer woman showed up. I remember that. I remember going to see her at the hotel. But then . . ." He shook his head. "I don't remember any of the rest of it, Hank. I'd ride out to look for Russ and then . . ."

"Sheriff," Hank said, urgency in his voice. "I've been hurt. Parrish is hurt, too, but he may still be alive. We've got to get help."

He lifted a hand to Knight, waited for the sheriff to take it and help him to his feet.

Knight shook his head. He took a step back. "I'm sorry, Hank, I truly am. But I can't go back to Bandera. Not this time. Not with all that innocent blood on my hands. It was different when it was Russ who was dead, but all those other folks . . ." His face twisted with emotion. "Tell Faye and Victoria that I'll always love them."

He raised the gun again.

Hank threw all his strength into lunging to his feet, but it wasn't enough. He was too damned late—

The gunshot sounded louder than ever, echoing back from the slopes of Bandera Pass.

In the last of the fading light, Hank managed to tear strips off his shirt and bind up the wound in his side. That stopped the bleeding. There was a flask of whiskey in the saddlebag of Whitaker's horse. Hank drank some of it and found enough strength to pull Parrish out from under the body of his horse. The young outlaw was out cold, had been ever since the fall. Whitaker was dead.

There had been no one to hear Sam Knight's story except Hank, no one to learn the truth.

And that was the way it would stay, Hank vowed. He tied Whitaker's body over the saddle of his horse, then found Sam Knight's mount in the trees and did the same for the sheriff. Parrish he somehow got upright in the saddle of his own horse and then climbed on behind him. That last effort had started the bullet tear in his side bleeding a little again, but it was just a slow trickle. Hank thought it would stop soon.

He took up the reins of the other two horses, then looped his other arm around Parrish. Maybe Parrish would live to hang, maybe he wouldn't. But Hank was going to do his best to bring him in alive.

He paused and looked around at the forbidding confines of the pass.

Sam Knight had fought his last gunfight here, and this time he had died a hero, helping to capture a pair of notorious desperadoes. That was the story Hank would tell, anyway. Knight's death would hurt Faye and Victoria, but not as much as the truth would.

Russ Knight could go back to being dead, and Susie Brewer could go on to wherever she had been headed when she arrived in Bandera. She would just have to wonder all over again what had happened to her outlaw lover. . . .

And Hank could go back to Austin, spin the same yarn to McNelly, wait for the captain to give him another job to do. That was one thing about being a Ranger. There was always another chore waiting for you.

Right now, Hank just hoped he could make it back to town without passing out. He thought he could.

He started the horses moving and rode away from Bandera Pass.